FULSOM JUSTICE

Rusty came at Kitchin like a clawing tiger. He was strong, and as fast as chain lightning, but he didn't have in his arms the seasoning of two years of hard labor like Kitchin did.

It was Fulsom Penitentiary that was fighting now—Fulsom, and the sight of "Blue Jay."

Rusty lunged again. Kitchin hit him away like a spinning top.

"Rusty," he said, "you're beat. I want you to take some time and come to. I'm going outside to wait till your head is cleared. This time it was fists; the next time it'll be guns. You get ready for the guns! Or else get ready to tell me that I'm the boss!"

Books by Max Brand

Ambush at Torture Canyon
The Bandit of the Black Hills
The Bells of San Filipo
Black Jack
Blood on the Trail
The Blue Jay
The Border Kid
Danger Trail
Dead or Alive
Destry Rides Again
The False Rider
Fightin' Fool
Fightin' Four
Flaming Irons
Ghost Rider (Original title: Clung)
Gunman's Reckoning
The Gun Tamer
Harrigan
Hired Guns
Hunted Riders
The Jackson Trail
Larramee's Ranch
The Longhorn Feud
The Longhorn's Ranch
The Long, Long Trail
The Man from Mustang
The Night Horseman
On the Trail of Four
The Outlaw

The Outlaw of Buffalo Flat
The Phantom Spy
Pillar Mountain
Pleasant Jim
The Reward
Ride the Wild Trail
Riders of the Plains
Rippon Rides Double
Rustlers of Beacon Creek
The Seven of Diamonds
Seven Trails
Shotgun Law
Silvertip's Search
Silvertip's Trap
Singing Guns
Single Jack
Six-Gun Country
Steve Train's Ordeal
The Stingaree
The Stolen Stallion
The Streak
The Tenderfoot
Thunder Moon
Tragedy Trail
Trouble Kid
The Untamed
Valley of Vanishing Men
Valley Thieves
Vengeance Trail

Published by POCKET BOOKS

Most Pocket Books are available at special quantity discounts for bulk purchases for sales promotions, premiums or fund raising. Special books or book excerpts can also be created to fit specific needs.

For details write the office of the Vice President of Special Markets, Pocket Books, 1230 Avenue of the Americas, New York, New York 10020.

MAX BRAND

THE BLUE JAY

PUBLISHED BY POCKET BOOKS NEW YORK

POCKET BOOKS, a division of Simon & Schuster, Inc.
1230 Avenue of the Americas, New York, N.Y. 10020

Copyright 1926 by Frederick Faust; copyright
renewed 1954 by Dorothy Faust

Published by arrangement with Dodd, Mead & Company, Inc.

ISBN: 0-671-54087-4

First Pocket Books printing April, 1978

10 9 8 7 6 5 4 3 2

POCKET and colophon are registered trademarks
of Simon & Schuster, Inc

Printed in the U.S.A

THE BLUE JAY

CHAPTER I

Nobody has to tell me. Because I know.

If I had stayed on the range, I would of been all right, because mixing around in my own crowd of folks, they would of understood that I was just extra happy and letting off steam. But you take a gang of city people, they got no sense of humor. Neither do they care none about what other folks would be thinking. The only street that they've any interest in is the one that they live on, and the only house of that street that amounts to a damn is the number where they stay.

I mean, the usual city folks. Not you! But you got to admit that the ordinary pavement walker is ornery.

I don't want to get mixed up. I want to tell this straight.

It begun with when I hit the pay dirt on the back of old Champion Mountain. I thought it would be one of those damn pinch veins. It started too good. But it *didn't* pinch. It strung out and got wider. I ground up a terrible lot of dust with my coffee mill and before that vein disappeared I had the haul of my life.

My haul was just too big. The idea of staying on the range or in a range town wouldn't fit up with a load of hard cash like that. I needed a lot fancier corral to show my stuff, and so I started for the City.

I didn't have no idea of spending everything that I had, of course. I figgered that my wad was so thick that I could paw at it for six months and never more than raise the surface. After that, I would go back to the range, where my own country is, and grab me a ranch and a gang of cows and start in reglar to be a real man. Prospecting was never more than a side show, to me.

When I got to town, I got myself fixed up with some clothes. They wasn't quiet, either. They was calculated to match up with the way that I was feeling inside, which was just gay, you understand? I didn't miss no tricks. Gloves and such went in with the lot and I had a vest that fair palpitated good cheer. I got me a cane, too— which they call them sticks when they speak polite. I even got down to spats, though I never got used to wearing cloth on my feet.

However, I want to say that where I appeared I was a noise that made folks look round, and I begun to have a real gay time. I set myself up at a hotel where you could spend five bucks for a meal without no particular pain and where the elevator boy looked like the son of a college president. After a while I collected some friends, too, and they showed me how really to part yourself from coin.

So I woke up one morning and pulled out my wad and I was pretty near beat to see that it had melted down to three hundred-dollar bills.

That wasn't enough to make a dent on the range. So I decided that it might as well go chasing after the rest of the gold dust. I rung up a couple of the boys and we started on a party.

I made my second big mistake before I started out. I was feeling a mite reckless but I figgered out that I wouldn't really want to hurt nobody's feelings, and so I left my Colt behind in the bureau drawer. That was sure a fool idea, as you'll see in a minute.

Anyway, we skidded around the town for a while and about midnight we found ourselves in a gambling joint. I seen my last twenty go across the green felt just at the same time that the dealer done a funny pass. I reached out and grabbed his hand, and down from his sleeve there come—oh, nothing much—just a couple of aces. You understand?

I was not really peeved. I had aimed to spend the last of my coin that night, and it didn't much matter how it went, but I seen that this discovery of mine give me a chance to make that party *real*. I just peeled off my coat and stood up on the table and told the folks in general what I thought of them and their ways. The boss of the joint, he sicked a couple of bounders on me, and so I dived off the table at them to make a beginning.

But they didn't make a beginning. They just flattened

out on the floor and I had to walk on their stomachs to get at the crowd. That's where the damage begun.

You see, if I had had the old Colt with me, there wouldn't of been any trouble. There rarely is with guns. Revolvers is not deadly weapons. They're just noise makers. Some folks fires off crackers on the Fourth; on the range, they're more partial to Colts. You get heated up and you pull your Colt and you blaze away. You don't hit nothing, because revolvers ain't meant for hitting targets except by accident. You just bust a couple of mirrors and windows and plough up the floor, and rake the ceiling, and everybody whoops and dances around and limbers up, and a good time is had by all and nothing in the way of damage done that a carpenter can't fix in half a day's work.

But I didn't have any Colt on me, as you've noticed in what I said before. All I had was my hands. And that was where I made my mistake.

I'm not small; and working a single jack and grinding pay dirt hadn't made me no smaller. When I stepped into that crowd and laid my hands on a couple of the boys, I could feel them give under my grip like their bones was made of India rubber. More than that, they got scared, and they begun to yell: "He's gone mad. Get the police!" It was disgusting to hear the way that they carried on because I was taking a mite of exercise. One of them got so excited that he hit me over the head with a chair, and after that I let that crowd have both fists. I waded through them across the room. Then I turned around and made a furrow back the long way of the place, and when I come to the door, there was a couple of cops.

What difference was cops to me? I bumped their heads together, took a breath of fresh air from the outside, and went back to finish scrambling up the eggs inside. But I'd hardly got started when one of the coppers crawled onto his feet and pulled a gun and I had to take it away from him. Then his buddy got funny with his night stick and busted it over my head, and I had to take him up and throw him through the window, with the glass and the frame carried along in front of him.

Then the lights went out, and right after that I skidded on something and went down on the back of my head. When I come to, I was riding on a wagon with a couple of boys in blue coats and brass buttons sitting on my chest and stomach. I says to them, would they please mind shifting off my stomach, and one of them says: "He's waking up. I told you that he would!"

"Sure," says another, "you can't kill a Swede by hitting him over the head. He ain't vulnerable there."

I says: "Gentlemen, did you sort of refer to me by speakin' of a Swede?"

They allowed that they did, and I got real irritated. The size of that patrol wagon, it cramped my style a good deal, but I managed to have a pretty good time, taking all things together, and the five coppers was pretty groggy when we got to the station-house. Then about a dozen fresh hands turned out and they grabbed me.

"Use gun-butts on him," says the sergeant, where he was lying on the floor holding his stomach with both arms. "Clubs ain't nothing but matchwood to him!"

That was a mighty practical police force. They took his word for it and they tried out my head with gun-butts. I come to in a cell with my head feeling like two, and all wrapped up in bandages. My clothes was tore up, too, which hurt me more than the feeling of my head—a whole lot! Because that outfit was something that the boys up there on the range would pretty near have paid admission for the sake of having a look at it!

However, the next morning I had to see the judge. He looked me over and wanted to know if I had resisted arrest, and the sergeant said that here was fifteen members of the force that would testify that I had and there was five more that he wanted particular to bring into the courtroom, but the doctor said that they was not fit to be allowed out of bed right then.

"And how about the prisoner?" said the judge. "He looks as though he had been sent down a flume!"

I said that I was all right and that I was sorry that I had messed up any of the boys.

"Are you a professional wrestler?" says the judge.

"With doggies and drills," says I.

The judge give me a grin. "You are just down from the range?" says he.

"My first and last appearance here, you bet," says I.

"All right," says the judge. "By the looks of my police force, it had *better* be your last appearance. Thirty days!"

"Thirty days?" sings out the police force, when they got me outside the room. "Thirty years would be more like it! I never hear an old sap like that judge. He had ought to be in an asylum for crippled brains!"

Thirty days didn't seem like very much, between you and me, but that was right where I made a terrible mistake. I thought that a month in jail would be nothing, but by the time that the first week was over, and the swellings and the bumps on my head had sunk down pretty near to the bedrock of my skull, my patience was all used up. Besides, the fare was pretty poor in that jail. It's hard to keep two hundred and twenty pounds of bone and meat working on the sort of a diet that they handed me. So the night of the eighth day, I tried the bars. I found a place where the stuff give a little when I pulled, and pretty soon I had worked a bar out of its socket.

My hands was bleeding before I got through working that bar loose, but after that, I had a sort of a can-opener to use on the rest of the prison. I never seen a lever that was handier for the forcing of doors than that bar was. It just worked fine, and I simply tore myself out of that jail, as easy as anything you would want.

I got to the street, when I remembered that my clothes wasn't any too good. I went back and tied up one of the guards and put on his suit and borrowed a hat from a peg on the wall of the office, and took a handful of smokes off the desk of the judge's room, and started out again.

I got eleven blocks and was due to make a clean break, when what should bump into me as I turned a corner but the night patrol! There was no reason why they should of suspected me. I was walking along brisk and sober, but they asked me what I was doing at that hour of the night, and when I started to tell them that I was a milk-wagon driver and that I was reporting for the morning beat, one of the coppers recognized my voice, and that patrol spilled all over me, yelling, "The Swede!"

My hands was sore from my work eight nights before, but I did pretty well until one of the flatties sank a forty-five calibre lug through my left thigh. They took me back and got me ready for the judge. It was pretty tough. The first time was just riot and resisting arrest, but this time it was breaking jail; assault on a guard; burglary; and resisting arrest all over again.

The judge says: "One year!"

Oh, why should I string this story out? I tried to bust

loose again, and the result was that I wound up in Fulsom for two years!

I don't know how it is now, but in those days, Fulsom was a nest of pretty hard birds. I was not any softy when I went into that penitentiary, but I was a hard-boiled, tool-proof bad one before I had been in there six months. The work was just hard enough to keep me fit and my appetite good enough to enjoy the prison grub—and I got meaner and harder all the time.

After I had served out a year of my sentence, I was headed for being a real bad one, but then I bumped into the chaplain. He went by the name of Maxim, and he was a rare good old boy with a white head and a cool blue eye. Him and me hit it off first class. We used to have boxing shows at the prison games, once a month, and that chaplain, he used to umpire the bouts. Says he, the first time that I showed, and when I was whaling the ribs out of a big two hundred and fifty pound Finn: "Kitchin," says the chaplain, breaking us out of a clinch, "you're not getting paid for this!"

That struck me funny, and I got to laughing so that I couldn't do the Finn no real harm, after that, aside from busting his nose in the last round. But the chaplain and me become friends. He got to talking to me regular and pretty soon he got me a soft job as a trusty, working in his office. It panned out pretty good, too, because when he called in a bad-actor it sort of helped the thug to take religion serious, seeing me in the background. I wasn't never a pretty man and having my head clipped didn't improve me none—it made my ears stick out most amazing.

The chaplain got me to reading books, too, and he educated me pretty thorough all round—which is why I can write so good about everything that I done and seen.

And when I left the prison, I was pretty near sorry to go. First of all, I had planned to go in with a couple of yeggs, and work the small towns in the back country with them, but the chaplain, he talked me out of it altogether. He said that the range was the place for me. And so, back to the range I went.

But none too proud. Jail-birds is not popular on the range. And I was known pretty well by my riding and by my being so big. But I looked over the map and I picked out a corner of the mountains where I had never been before. I picked out the town specially because it had such a funny name, which was Sour City. And three days later, I crawled out from the rods and stretched myself and looked over my new country.

It was a pretty good little town. It was set down in the corner between where Sour Creek runs into the Big Muddy. It wasn't any "sour" city, either. It was as neat a little town as you'd ever like to see, with some paving, and street lamps, and good shops, and one brick hotel and two that wasn't brick, and pretty nearly everything that anybody could want to have in a town. Over the hills that rolled up all around there was a fine big sweep of cattle country, and behind that the mountains went sashaying up to the sky with black pines most of the way, and a white-headed summit, here and there.

Altogether, it looked good to me. I stopped in at a blacksmith shop to see for a job, but they was full handed; anyway, they couldn't see past my peeled head, and so I went out on the street and the first person that I bumped into was the sergeant—I mean, the police sergeant that I had laid out in the patrol wagon down in the city!

CHAPTER II

Aiming the way that I was towards starting at the bottom·
and working my way up, with a new name the same as
the chaplain had planned for me to take, I wasn't any
too tickled to see the face of that sergeant, of course,
but I was plumb happy compared with him.

He give me a wall-eyed look and then he side-stepped
right out into the gutter. I started to pass on, but then I
changed my mind and turned around and I went back to
where he was still standing and looking back at me. He
acted like he expected me to hit him.

"I'm armed, Kitchin," says he. "Don't try nothing! I'm
armed and I won't take anything from you!"

"Sergeant," says I, "you got me wrong!"

He put up his hand quick. "I'm not a sergeant, any
more," says he. "I'm doing some ranching up here, Blondy,
and it don't help any to bring up the past!"

I hadn't liked him when I met him back there in the
city, because he took it to heart so mean, the way that I
laid him out in the patrol wagon. Now I could see that he
was even worse than I had thought.

You take them by and large, the cops are a pretty good
lot. Here and there you may run across a rotter, of course.
Here and there you'll find a pretty bad grafter who plays
in with the crooks; but it's never as bad as the newspapers
would like to make out, I've always thought. A policeman, he's a fellow that is willing to risk his life for his
job, and mostly men that do that sort of work have got to
have something that is worth while in them. Take most of
those boys down there in the city, they didn't hold no
grudge against me because I had spoiled a few of their

14

faces for a while. One fellow that had a nose out of place used to make a point of coming around to see me, and he used to chat with me, real cheerful. He would tell me how that he was taking boxing lessons, and how he hoped that when I got out of jail, I would drop around to see him, and then he would peel off his uniform and him and me would have it out, and he would try to do for my nose what I had already done for *his*. I intended to give him the chance, too, and if things ever get laid so that I can take some time off and get back to that time, I'm sure going to call on him and give him his chance at me.

Well, most coppers are that way—clean, hard-hitters—but now and then you'll come across an exception to the rule. That sergeant had got a busted rib where I hit him in the police patrol. Not really clean busted, but only fractured; nothing hardly worth speaking about at all, between men, but he laid on about it a lot, and he used to come and tell me that when I got out of that jail, I would be lucky if he didn't have me in again so fast that my head would swim!

Now, all of these things come piling back through my head when I met him up there in Sour City. I seen where he hated to have it known that he had ever been a sergeant, because he felt that he had raised himself a whole long ways above those old days, and that made me dislike him a lot more than I ever had before. Because about the lowest thing that a man can do is try to cut himself loose from what he used to be in his past.

I says: "Randal, if you want me to forget that you used to be a police sergeant—"

"That's exactly what I want you to do!" says he. He was pretty eager about it, too. "However," he went right on, "I don't suppose that you're going to be staying around Sour City very long?"

The minute that I seen him, I had decided that I would be moving on as soon as the next freight pulled out from the station, but the way he talked, it made me think that maybe I had better stay on right where I was. It looked like a chance was opening up; and I decided to talk straight to him. The chaplain, he had pretty well persuaded me that you don't gain anything by talking around the corners about folks.

I says: "Randal, it ain't hard to see that you want to get rid of me, from here?"

"Not at all!" says he, and he waved his hand; but I could see a fairly sick look on his face. I knew that I was weighing on his mind, pretty bad.

I says: "Now, Randal, you've got and worked yourself up to where you're a rancher that can afford to wear real solid silver spurs, as I see, and handmade boots, and all the rest, and you ain't fond of the idea of having the folks around here ever know that you used to wear a night stick, quite a bit."

"You may put it that way," says he. "I really welcome frank talk!"

"The hell you do!" says I, "but you're gunna get it! I don't like you, Randal, and I never did. You was low and mean and ornery, and there ain't hardly anything in the world that would do me so much good as to sink a hand in your ribs again!"

He give a little grunt and a step back, at that.

"But," says I, "I know what I can do and what I can't. And what I can't do is to make any more trouble. I've had my dose. I've been licked good and proper and I ain't gunna forget it. *Nothing* is ever gunna give the law a chance to send me back to Fulsom, again. Now, Randal, I'm up here not on a bat, the way that you seen me down in town, but mighty quiet and sober. I'm a hard-working man, and I want to get a job and I want to stick to it. You understand? Now, the folks around here ain't any too fond of employing jail-birds, and you know it. And the easiest thing in the world would be to get me out of this section of the country by just letting the word get out that I've been serving a prison sentence. But the minute that I hear any talk like that, I'm gunna know who started it, and I'm gunna come for you. And when I get to you, I'm gunna forget all about prison. If they get me and send me back on account of you and that sort of talk, it'll be murder, Randal—and I mean it!"

I did mean it, too. Because when I thought of losing a chance to go straight on account of a rat like this here Randal, it fair sickened me. I would like to of wrung his neck right then and there. But Randal understood me. He was pretty grey as he stared at me. Then he begun to nod. He had a long, thin face with deep-set eyes, and now an idea begun to work up in those eyes. All at once, he fetched a hand into a vest pocket and brought out a wallet and he sifted a few bills out of the leather. He holds it out to me.

"Here's seventy-five dollars," says he.

"And that's my price for beating it and keeping my mouth shut?" says I. "I'll see you in hell first, Randal. Your money is dirt, to me!"

That was pretty free and independent talking, and in more than one part of the range that I could name, it would of got a man shot, right there and on the spot, but it looked like this was not one of them parts of the range. Randal, he just smiled back at me.

He said: "Now, don't you be a damn fool, Blondy. The thing for you to do, kid, is to step into that store up the street and get yourself a suit of clothes. They've got a big assortment, and maybe they'll have a suit that'll fit you. They carry hats and shoes, too, and shirts and neckties. You haven't got enough money there to buy the world, but you got enough to fit yourself out decently. Well, Blondy, that's what I want you to do, and after you get yourself made up, you come over to the hotel, and you'll find me waiting for you in the lobby. It'll be lunch time, then, and you and me will go in and surround some chops, or whatever looks good to you in the eating line. You do what I tell you, and don't ask any questions until it's all over."

I shouldn't of taken that money, of course. Looking back on it, I can see that I was a fool and sort of a crook to take it, but I'll give you my word that it wasn't the idea of getting something for nothing that appealed to me so much. What flabbergasted me, really, was the mystery that was behind all of this, because, mind you, this ex-sergeant of police wasn't any extravagant, generous sort of fellow. I aim to believe that you can mostly spot a generous man by a sort of a stupid wall-eyed look that he has. You try your hand at it. Just look over the men that you know and you'll see what I mean quick enough, because the tight-fisted fellows are apt to have a pretty wideawake look—as if they were trying to make out whether you were worth noticing or not—but the generous folks have a sort of a stupid look. When you ask them for something they get a sort of a sick expression.

Now there wasn't anything stupid about this here fellow Randal. He was as sharp as a rat. There was something up his sleeve. He wanted to get something out of it, and I naturally wondered what it could be. It was a case of my wits against his wits, and I was willing to bet that my brains were as hard as my fist, so far as he was concerned. I decided that I would do what he said. I went up the street to a store and by the grace of God I found out a pretty good-looking brown suit and I got right into it. There was a hard job finding shoes that would fit, but I managed it at last after a pretty tight squeeze, and I sashayed out of that place with a new hat on the side of my head, looking like a new million, you bet.

I found the ex-sergeant in the lobby of the hotel and he give me one squint up and down and nodded:

"You take to it easy," said he. "You got a knack for spending, I see."

Then he led me into the dining-room and we settled down to see how much food could be got onto one table, and after that, we seen just how quick that table could be emptied again. And so pretty soon he came around to cigar time and set back and clamped his teeth in a nice-looking black cigar. But I stuck to cigarettes that I rolled myself, because I wanted to keep my head clear.

CHAPTER III

He said: "Now, big boy, you figure that this is all pretty queer, and after I've handed out enough money to dress you up, you wonder what I'm going to try to get out of you. Ain't that right?"

"I dunno," says I, "but maybe it's just because you're a nacherally generous chap and you're willing to let bygones be bygones."

Because, you see, I wanted to bluff him out and make him think that I was about ten shades simpler than the fact. But he just leaned a bit over the table and puffed out a cloud of smoke and grinned at me through it.

"You lie like hell!" says he.

And I couldn't help grinning back.

"Maybe you and me are gunna be able to understand each other," says I.

"I guess we are," says he. "I *hope* that we are. But the first thing for you to write down in red is that I haven't forgot a thing. I still wear a strip of tape on my side where you busted me in the ribs, and after I take that tape off, I'll still remember. I'm not a friend of yours, big boy, and don't you forget it."

"Randal," says I, "for a crook, you talk like an honest man. You sort of warm up my heart. Now start going and spill the beans. You want my scalp, and you've bought me a new outfit. When do you pull the knife?"

He grinned again. He seemed to like this aboveboard talk as much as I did. Then he said: "I don't know when the scalping will take place. You're a pretty hard one, Kitchin, and I don't know just how I'll be able to go about cracking you. But in the meantime, I have to forget

19

about what I want to do to you. I have to think just about what you can do for me."

"Go on," says I. "This sounds all better and better, I got to admit. Where does the music and the dancing begin?"

"Poison is bad stuff," says he, "but when you want to get rid of the ground squirrels, it has its uses—and you're the poison that I want to use now. You hear me talk?"

"I hear you talk. You got a poison job and I'm to be the goat. Go ahead!"

"That's exactly it," says Randal, working into the fat of his cigar and enjoying it with his eyes half closed. "I've got a bad job on my hands and I need somebody like you. But first, I have to put the cards on the table. Not that I want to, but that I have to in order to get you interested."

I nodded. It looked pretty clear that he was talking honest. Not because he liked honesty, but because he saw that it was the only policy that would work in this case.

So he went on to say that he had come out of a family where everybody was pretty well fixed, and that when he was a youngster, just out of college, his dad had set him up in business and given him a flying start. But his ways weren't saving ways. He liked the things that money give you but he didn't cotton to the ways that money is made. So, pretty soon, he went bust.

Right about then, his father went on the rocks, too, and it busted the old man's heart. He died and there was nothing in the estate for young Randal, so he looked around and got him a job on the side in the police force of the big town, without letting any of his family know what he was doing. Maybe it was take a thief to catch a thief. Anyway, he done pretty good as a policeman and worked up to a pretty good job as a sergeant, when he got word that his dad's brother, Stephen Randal, had died, and lacking any other heirs that he was fond of, had split his cash between Harry Randal's brother and sister and what he left to Harry (my friend) was his ranch.

It was a going ranch and very prosperous, and when Harry had a look at it, he felt that everything was pretty fine for him. Then, about a month after he took possession, over came his grandfather, Henry Randal.

Says the ex-sergeant: "This old goat, my grandfather,

is one of those foxes that lose their strength when they get old but that don't lose their wits, y'understand? He has about three millions in land and money, and when he visited me, he opened up and showed me his bank account and the statement of the stocks and the loans that he had outstanding. It was a list as long as your arm, I tell you! He said to me:

" 'Harry, I think that you're a bright boy, but I don't know about your working qualities. This ranch of your uncle's was always a hard proposition to make pay. Your uncle did well here because your uncle was a man who worked about twenty hours out of every day. One reason that this ranch is hard to make pay is that, though the grass is good here and there is plenty of water for the cows, the ranch backs up on a regular hole in the wall country, and it's pretty hard to keep the rustlers from edging in and getting away with the cream of the calf crop every year. Your uncle Stephen managed to scare the rustlers off because he was a hard-boiled fellow, as maybe you know, and they feared him morning night and noon, and don't you forget it! But, Harry, I don't know that you're going to do so well. You are bright, but I don't see you working twenty hours out of every twenty-four. You are brave enough, but I don't know that you'll make the rustlers lose any sleep. So you see that I understand what troubles you have ahead of you.

" 'Now, Harry, I've showed you a property worth three millions. I can go another step and tell you something else, and that is that I don't like your brother. He's gone in for a banking job in a city; and I hate the cities and the people that stay in them. Your sister has married a fat-head who doesn't know enough to come in out of the rain. And neither of them are going to get a penny of my money. That leaves you, Harry, as the sole natural heir, so far as I'm concerned! But, mind you, I have a lot of doubts about you; and the way that you can clear those doubts up is to take hold on this ranch and make a paying proposition out of it. Every quarter I'm going to send out an expert accountant that I can trust to go over your books, and if those books don't balance on the right side, you'll hear from me to the effect that you needn't worry about your inheritance any more. But, Harry, if you can take hold of that ranch and work it satisfactorily to me—and well enough to make a real profit out of it,—you are going to get every penny of my money. You understand? I have a heart that is due to stop working in about a year or two. I haven't any illusions about my future, at all. I'll die within about twelve months or two years, at the outside, and I want to leave my fortune in one lump to a man who can take good care of it. Think it all over, my boy, and when you've finished thinking, start in and work like the devil. You have to have patience, courage, and brains, and strength to win out. What your other moral qualities may be, I don't know, and I don't give a damn —I'm not any saint, myself—but if you can make this ranch pay, you're as good a man as your uncle Stephen was, and he was my favorite son.'

"Right there he finished. He wouldn't stay to dinner. He got onto his horse in spite of his eighty years and his bad heart and he rode twenty-five miles back to his own ranch. And there you are, Kitchin. You know me. You think I'm a crook. Maybe I am. I know you. I know you're a crook, too, and there hasn't been time for you to let your hair grow since you got out of the pen. Besides that, you hate me because I made things hard for you in the jail, and I hate you because you broke a rib for me and fractured a good deal of my self-respect. Very well. Let's look at the other side of the picture.

"You're broke. You need a job. You know the cattle country and the cattle business. I got that much out of you, listening to you in the jail. On the other hand, I'm in a bad boat. I have a big ranch, and I've loaded up my staff of cow punchers with regular two-gun bad-men —hard-boiled eggs with reputations that need a short-hand reporter working a week to write them up. I got those hard fellows because I wanted to run out the rustlers in the backcountry. You see? But now that I've got them in, I've found out that they work hand in glove with the rustlers themselves. At least, that's my suspicion. I dread the next round up, because I know that it's going to show me short of hundreds of cows—and that will be where my pretty dream busts all to pieces and the three million goes up in smoke.

"I got my place full of these hard-boiled fellows, but now that I have them, I can't run them. If I fire them, they'll simply go over to the rustlers and I'll be in worse than ever. Fire one, and they'll all quit, because they're as thick as thieves. I can't show my face in the bunk-house without getting laughed at, now. I've hired three ranch-managers in the last three weeks, and not one of them has lasted twenty-four hours with that crew of yeggs.

"Very well. What I want is a two-fisted, two-gun fight-ing fool who will beat that crowd into order and make them like it! I'm willing to take a long chance and try you out. I'm desperate, and that ugly mug of yours looks good to me, right now. What do you say, young feller? What do you say to taking on the job, Kitchin?"

I rolled this idea over my tongue. It sounded good and it sounded bad. I had my two hands, and they were pretty strong hands. What with the life I had led, and the last two years of hard labor in the prison, with box-ing every week, I was as hard as nails, and there was two hundred and twenty pounds of me to be hard. No, I didn't worry about what would happen if it came to a hand-to-hand rough and tumble mix-up. But where would I be if the guns were pulled? I was never any hand at guns, as you may have gathered from what I've said about revolvers before, and if some handy two-gun dick was to bob up in a nasty humor, where would I be? Nowhere, of course! However, there is nothing like a hard job to make you rise out of yourself. This looked to me like a lost cause, and there is enough Irish in me to make me like lost causes.

What I couldn't really do, I might be able to bluff through. I said to Randal:

"Well, where do I get off? I get a year or so of bullet-eating, and fighting and excitement. And after that—?"

"I'm glad to see that you're a practical man with an eye on the future, old son," says this Randal. "I'm *mighty* glad to see it. It proves to me more than ever that you and me *will* get on. And now, what do you say your reward ought to be?"

I thought it over. As the copybooks say, there ain't anything like hitching your wagon to a star.

I said: "It looks to me like your main job is being a grandson, and my main job is everything else. Well, Randal, I suppose that the best that I can ask from a hard customer like you is a fifty-fifty split."

Randal grinned. "You get half of the three million and I get the other half?" he says, very soft.

"That's about it," said I.

He shook his head. "Guess again. No, I'll make you a proposition and a big one. That ranch I'm on is a damned good thing—for the right man. Uncle Stephen cleared fifty thousand a year for the last ten years that he was on it. Now, old timer, what I say is that if you can make the ranch pay for me, you can make it pay for yourself, and if this game works, I take the three millions, of course, and you get the ranch. You can't budge me a cent higher than that!"

I knew he meant what he said. I leaned back in the chair and sighed.

"All right," said I. "Put that in writing, and—I'm ready for a cigar, now!"

CHAPTER IV

He didn't like the idea of putting a contract like that in writing. As he pointed out, I could use that contract to extract blackmail out of him, in case I threw up the overseer job on the ranch. But I showed him that in case I couldn't make a go of the thing, I wouldn't be able to get much out of him. The only opinion he had to be afraid of was his grandfather's and the only person that could let him win his grandfather's respect—and money—was me.

Randal thought it all over very slowly, his eyes fixed on a far corner of the room, but not a shadow of a frown on his face. I could tell that he was a deep one by that. Your simple chap will wrinkle his face into a knot when he's working out a problem, but your real deep one never bats an eye. Finally Randal looks me in the eye:

"Old timer," says he, "I think that you're about as downright bad a case as—I am!"

"You flatter me," says I. "But does the thing go through?"

"It goes through as slick as a whistle," says he. "I'm putting all my dice in this one box and I can't keep any up my sleeve. So here goes!"

He pulled an old envelope out of his pocket and he tore it open, and on the two sides of it, in a fine, clerical hand, he wrote out that contract, and signed it and passed it over to me.

Of course he hadn't missed a chance to put in some 'if's and 'buts' that changed the whole meaning, but I had him cross them out and then that contract made slick reading, for me. When I folded it up and shoved it into my wallet, I asked him what the next stage was to be, and he said that we had to get ready to go out to the ranch. The reason that he had bought me the new suit was partly because he wanted to open my mind and get me prepared for something big to come, and partly because I would have to make a pretty good impression on the boys at the ranch, because if I walked in on them dressed like a tramp, they wouldn't respect me none.

There was good sense in that, of course. They say that clothes don't make the man, but I've noticed that from your best girl up to the gent that you touch for a loan, the clothes you wear make the difference between getting inside the door and being left out in the cold.

The idea of Randal was that I should lay hold of a suitcase, buy some stuff to put in it, and then drive out with him in the buckboard. I agreed that that was a pretty good idea. He had some business to attend to, and so I said that I would go out and do the buying, and I asked him what money he wanted to let me have.

He fair staggered me, at that. He pulled out a wad of money and told me to go as far as that would take me. When I counted the wad, there was five hundred in it!

I could see that Randal didn't figure me for any piker that would be apt to take my money and my clothes and board the first train out of the town. He expected that I would try for the big game, and I decided that I would show him that he wasn't wrong in trusting me to play for the main graft.

I went down to the Mexican quarter of Sour City; that is to say, on the northern side of the creek, where the water put an end to the white-man's town and let the greasers begin. I wanted to try the Mexicans for the stuff that I needed, because I knew that in that part of the town I was more apt to find stuff such as I wanted; also, what happens among greasers doesn't float back to the whites—it's dead and buried right where it happened—and I didn't want to have any curious eyes watching me and reporting me so's the boys out on the ranch might hear about it.

The white side of Sour City was as slick as you please, all dressed up with shiny pavements, and such, but

across the creek, you wouldn't believe what a difference!
Nothing but twelve inches of dust in the streets, with
the wind stirring up drifts and pools in it, all the time,
and when a horse galloped in that part of the town, he
left a regular fog behind him, as high as the tops of the
houses. Everything was dirty, and broken down, and
lazy, and comfortable. In the doorways, you would see
the old greasy señoras setting and patting out their sup-
ply of tortillas for that evening. And here and there a
couple of pigs would be squealing at each other while they
tried to root at the same spot in the dirt. And there
was kids around that wasn't bothered much with clothes;
mostly a shirt or a pair of trousers, but not the two together at the same time. But everybody looked happy
and sort of in tune with things.

I seen a great big store where there was new stuff
and second hand, everything that a body could want or
even think of. All along the front of the veranda, on
pegs and nails, there was old saddles, bridles, quirts,
spurs, chaps, stirrup leathers, stirrups, and saddle flaps,
saddle-bags, pack-saddles, and blackwhips, and black-
snakes, and four-hoss lashes, with bits in a thousand
fancy Mexican styles for the torturing of a good hoss;
and all the spurs different too. That was the sort of a
store that a kid could stand in front of and wish for a
whole year together—and make a new wish every ten
seconds!

There was a kid there, too. He was a slim-built brat
about thirteen or fourteen. His voice hadn't changed yet.
It was high and thin, but it hadn't begun to crack yet.
It was more like a woman's. He was pretty ragged, but
anyway he had enough clothes of one sort or another to
cover him down to the calves of the legs. He wore huarachos—wood, of course—and he had a battered old
felt hat jammed down on a head that was covered with
an extra thick thatching of black hair.

He held out his hand before me and asked me, with
his head onto one side and his voice whining, would I
please help a poor orphan what had no father nor no
mama, so he could get a little to buy a loaf of bread,
which he would eat it with cold water and bless the God
that sent me along to relieve the poor.

"Ain't you got a cent on you, kid?" says I.

"Ah, señor! Alas, señor, there has been no kindness here to-day!"

I reached down and grabbed him by the ankles and heaved him up into the air. Out from his pockets come a rain of silver and coppers that rattled on the floor of the veranda of the store, and some of the coins rolled into the deep dust of the street, and a few of them slipped down through the cracks in the boards. Then I give him a toss to one side and he spun through the air and looked as though he was going to land on his head. But he didn't, because he was as active as a cat. He righted himself while he was still sailing through the air and hit the ground on hands and feet.

He was a surprise, that little scalawag. Instead of bursting out into boohooing because he'd lost all that money, he ripped a couple of man-sized Spanish cuss-words at me, and a voice behind me said: "Jump, señor!"

I didn't wait to ask why I ought to jump. I did it, and got back through the door of the store just as a wink of light come jump through the air where I had been standing, and there was a knife sticking into the door jamb and humming like a overgrown hornet.

"That Pepillo ees wan devil, no?" says the store-keeper.

"Say it in Spanish," says I, "I know the lingo."

"He will hang soon," says the storekeeper, in Spanish.

But he didn't seem to take the kid serious in spite of the knife. He just stood up there and grinned out at the street where Pepillo was ferreting the coins out of the dust.

He kept one eye on his work and the other eye on me, all the time, and he talked, too, with hand and tongue— he was sure ambidextrous. To give you some idea of the language that that kid was capable of, leaving out all the high spots that might hurt your ears if they're sensitive to such stuff: "Gringo dog," says this Pepillo, "one night I shall come where you sleep and put a knife between your ribs. Or perhaps I shall rip up your belly, son of a thief! Come out, coward, to fight with me. For I have still another knife! I do not fear you! Come, pigface!"

I pulled the knife out of the wood where he had stuck it and I threw it back into the dust.

"You little snake," says I, "does your mama know what you're about?"

"My mama watches me from the blue Heaven and puts a curse on all gringo dogs," says this kid. "The devils will roast you for ten thousand years on a white fire and stick spits through your middle to turn you over the flames!"

I heard the storekeeper chuckling behind me. Matter of fact, I couldn't help laughing, too, there was so damn much venom in that kid and there was so little fear in him, too.

He reached for the knife that I had thrown down into the dust in front of him, and I waved my arm so that the shadow swung over him. Well, sir, the way that kid side-stepped out of the way of any chance of danger was a caution. He chucked his knife almost with his back turned to me, I thought, and the damn blade skinned along a quarter of an inch from my temple. Another bit in, and it would of slipped through my eye into my brain and that would of been the end of Blondy Kitchin and this here yarn.

I dunno why I wasn't madder or more scared, but that kid just tickled me, really. For one thing, he was so doggone handsome, which you wouldn't believe it! And then again, as he stood there ripping out cusses and telling me where I was bound to go when I went west, his voice had a sort of a sweetness to it—like a bird, only a bird that was singing very mad. Yes, he tickled me all over, more'n any kid that I ever seen before. First thing that I knew, I'd grabbed a dollar out of my pocket and heaved it at his head.

He put up his hand and snatched the flash of that coin out of the air and he stood there looking down to it in his palm. I dunno that ever he had seen a whole dollar before, by the look on his face, and the way that he said: "Dios! Dios! Dios!" over and over. You would of thought that I had handed him a ticket to Heaven.

CHAPTER V

"What is your name?" says I to the storekeeper.

"Gregorio," says he. "I am Gregorio, son of Pedro Oñate—"

"Hold on, Gregorio," says I. "I just want a name to call you by and not a song to sing to you!"

"Ah, well, señor!" says he. But he was pretty good-natured. It was plain that he was sort of tickled by me giving the dollar to the kid after the knife-heaving.

"Have you got any saddles, here?" says I.

"Señor!" says he, and he waves to the front of the store, where there was a whole mob of them saddles.

"Sure," says I, "they're leather to sit in, but have you got any *saddles?*"

He give me a look. You see, a fancy saddle is about one-half of a Mexican's life.

"Señor," says he, "as one gentleman to another, I shall show you a saddle which any *caballero* would be proud to sit in."

He goes back in the store and pretty soon he brings out a humdinger, all set over with silver what-nots. I give it a look and it sounded to me. What I wanted to do, was to walk out there to the bunkhouse on that ranch not like a fancy tramp, but with a gun and a saddle on me, like I really belonged on the range, and like I had done something that was worth while, on the range. A good saddle would be a pretty fair proof of it. This here saddle was a corker, all worked with fine carvings, and covered with polished silver that pretty near dazzled you just to look at it.

"How much?" says I.

Gregorio closed his eyes.

"Ah," says he, "when I think how much I gave for it! But no—I can never hope to get that much out of it! Besides, I like you, señor, and for my friends, I have no thought. Money does not exist. To you, then, señor, I give this saddle away—for four hundred dollars!"

It gave me a start, the naming of a price like that for just a saddle, but when I come to look at the thing closer, and fingered it, I felt like I had to have it, because I was pretty sure that a saddle like that would show those hard-eggs on the Randal ranch that I was no freezeout or bluffer.

Just then a little voice pipes up at my shoulder: "Mas sabe el loco en su casa, que el cuerda en la ajena." Which is one of them neat Spanish proverbs: and it means, in case you don't know Spanish, that a fool in his own house knows a lot more than a wise man does away from home.

I looked around and there was that Pepillo. He had kicked off his wooden huarachos and so he had sneaked into the store without making no noise in his bare feet.

Gregorio had seemed to like the kid well enough when he seen him in the street, but inside of the store, it was a different story.

"Little thief, and son of a thief," yells Gregorio. "Have I not told you that if I found you in my store again—"

He laid a hand on the counter, like he would jump over and squash that kid flat, but Pepillo just stood where he was, and he lifted up one foot and scratched the heel of it on his other shin. You would be surprised to see his feet, they was so small and so soft, pretty near like a baby's. It made me see how young he was. He sticks out his chin and he makes a face at Gregorio.

"Old fat fool!" says he. "Do you think that I fear you when I have found a friend such as this señor?" And he puts his arm through mine, as free as you please.

Well, I was plumb tickled. It gives me a sort of a nice warm feeling all over, though I knew that the little devil, he was just throwing a bluff to work me and keep a high hand over Gregorio. Gregorio got madder than ever, but he looked from the kid to me.

He says: "Do not be deceived, señor. This little rat, for a whole fortnight he has been in this city making friends and using them and losing them again when he is through with them. The little thief has a charm in his hands. He steals a watch while you smile at him!"

I looked down at the kid. "Look here, Pepillo, d'you steal?"

Well, he cocks his head up and looks at me plumb trusting out of them big brown eyes of his—or was they black? I never can make out. He says: "Si, señor?"

"What!" I yells at him. "Are you a thief?"

"Si, señor," says he, as cool as a waterlily. "And what I steal, I sell to this Gregorio."

Gregorio ripped out a couple of volleys of cusses and reached for a blacksnake, but his face was pretty red and I guessed that there must be something in what the kid had said.

"Leave Pepillo be," says I, "and let's get on with the saddle. What do you know about this here saddle, Pepillo?"

"I know the gentleman who sold it to Gregorio," says Pepillo.

"It is a lie!" says Gregorio, but he looks pretty sick.

"He was very ill, that gentleman," says Pepillo. "He has sold everything except this one saddle. He asked five hundred dollars for it and said that it cost him a thousand, but Gregorio said that who will buy a used saddle that another man has sat in? And he bought the saddle for eighty dollars!"

"When I come to die—" begins Gregorio, very solemn.

"Here, Gregorio," I busts in, "you and me want to do some business, but we ain't got any extra time on our hands. I'll give you a hundred and fifty dollars for that saddle. That's pretty near a hundred per cent on your investment."

"When a rat squeaks, do you believe it?" says Gregorio. "This boy is the son of the devil, and all the city knows it. I should be bankrupt if I—"

"Put the saddle away, then," says I. "There's a thirty-dollar saddle at the door that would suit me good enough—"

He picks up the saddle but his motions are pretty slow, and finally he says: "Amigo mio, though I lose money dreadfully, still I should like to see a true *caballero* sitting in this saddle, and is there any man as worthy as you, my dear friend? No, you shall have it—for two hundred dollars!"

Well, it was worth that money and a lot more—just the silver work would of cost a lot more—so I paid the cash, though Pepillo groaned and wiggled, and said that it was robbery. He had saved me two hundred on the price, at that.

Next I got me a big leather carryall; one of them expansible things that you can crowd everything into up to a whole hoss. I bought me enough junk to pretty well fill it out, and everything was amazing cheap. Then it come to guns, and I had Gregorio show me a whole rack filled with Colts. I looked them all over. Matter of fact, they was all new-looking and very fine, but new looks wasn't what I wanted. I pretended to try them all and not to like the balance of them.

"Gregorio," said I, "I ask for a gun, but I mean that I wish to have a friend that can be relied upon. Do you understand?"

He understood nearly everything, that Gregorio, and now he squinted at me. He hesitated for a long time.

"Señor," said he, "you have been a good customer. Here is a little treasure that I have been keeping for myself. But what can a man keep from a good friend? Here is a gun which has been proved; I dare not say by whom!"

And he pulled out from his own clothes an old-fashioned Colt. He handed it to me and I give it a look. It had a wooden handle that was black with time and with sweat and polished by a lot of fingering. I looked it all over. And finally, on the underside of the barrel, I seen seven little notches that had been filed into the good steel.

I knew what that meant. This here gun had killed seven men. And it had just that sort of a mean look, I can tell you. It couldn't of been more to my taste. I wanted to tote a gun along with me that would look pretty bad and dangerous to the boys out there on the ranch, if they was to see it. And what could I of found more than this?

Gregorio wanted forty dollars, which was highway robbery for an old gun like that, but I had to pay twenty-five before I could get it—and the luck that went along with it.

"Because," whispered Gregorio, "the señor who owned this gun after all died in a peaceful sick bed. Is it not strange?"

It suited me. I stowed the gun away and carried my saddle and carryall out to the veranda, while Gregorio went to get me a buckboard that would take my stuff around to the hotel. Pepillo waited with me on the veranda. I handed him a five-dollar bill, which was small pay for all the money that he had saved me in the store. He looked at the bill without a lot of interest, I thought, seeing how one dollar had seemed to mean so much to him before.

"Ah, well, señor," says he, "you are to go away, then?"

"And you, Pepillo?" says I.

"God knows, señor," says he. "But it will be a long time before I meet another of whom I am afraid."

"Hey!" says I. "You mean that you're afraid of me?"

"Por Dios!" says Pepillo. "My ankles still burn like fire where you caught them. The devil is in those big hands of yours. Why should I not fear you? If I cursed you and threw knives—that was only a greater token that I feared you the more!"

He was a puzzler, that kid. I took to him a lot, I can tell you, and by the sick sort of a way that he opened his eyes and looked up to me, you would of thought that he was feeling pretty bad, too. Gregorio come around the corner with the buckboard.

"Gregorio," I hollered all at once, "give this boy some clothes and shoes and such and fix him up. He is my *mozo;* he goes with me!"

CHAPTER VI

Well, that speech came bursting out of me, as you might say, out of the largeness of the heart. I felt as though I was offering somebody the world. I guess that I expected this here young Pepillo to fall on his knees, or something, and give thanks for what I intended to do for him. Well, he didn't. He hauls off and gives me an ugly eye. He says:

"What mozo?"

"Why," says I, "you, of course."

"Me?" says Pepillo, waving his eyebrows up to the top of his forehead and jabbing his thumb into his breast. "Did you say Pepillo?"

"Sure," says I. "I've sort of took a fancy to you. I'm gonna make you, kid. I'm gunna dress you up like you was a millionaire. I'm gunna make you look like a gentleman!"

You should of seen his face. It went sort of black.

"Ha! Ha!" says Pepillo, trying to laugh, but only choking. "It is a good joke. Por Dios, I laugh—I laugh. *You* are to make a gentleman of me. You are to make me a—it is too much! And I am the son of—"

He stopped himself with such an effort that his teeth barely clicked in time to shut back the word and his lips remained grinning back, so that on my word, he looked like a damned young wolf.

"You are the son of who?" says I.

"Your master, gringo swine!" says this young brat, and he pours out a stream of Spanish cussing that fair made my hair rise. You could say this for that Pepillo's system of cussing: he didn't leave nothing out, but he

35

started right in at the beginning and he traced all my
family tree, and you can bet that it was a thorn tree!

Now I tell you true, if any other kid this side of hell
had tried to hand such a line of talk to me, I would of
tied him up and skinned him alive as a starter, and after
that I would of taught him manners while he was raw.
But Pepillo was different. Right in the midst of his
cussing and his raging and his raving, it was sort of en-
tertaining, if you know what I mean. If you had been
there to watch him you would of said that the graceful
way he had was like a bird putting its head from side to
side while it sung as though it would bust its heart.

Pepillo was that way; like a singing bird. That voice of
his wasn't never nothing but musical. It was a sort of
a pleasure to be damned by Pepillo. When he cussed, it
wasn't any ordinary cussing, either. He used his wits and
made it interesting. I wish that I could remember exactly
how he would light in and dress anybody down, but his
tongue moved just a shade faster than my thoughts
could travel, and so he was always a jump around the
corner from my memory.

"All right, Pepillo," says I. "I am a gringo swine while
there is nobody else around but you and me. You savvy?
But the minute that another gent hears you using language like that on me, I'll right up and break you in
two!"

He seemed to like that idea. He stopped cussing and
began to laugh at me and at the whole idea, and you
could see that he was tickled all over.

"Then, señor," says he, "you would have me to be
your mozo, and what would you do for me?"

"I would keep you in decent clothes," says I. "I would
see that you got a chance at schooling, even if I had to
teach you myself—"

Pepillo puts back his head and laughs again. Doggone
me if it wasn't a queer sensation to let myself be laughed
at by anybody, particularly by a little runt of a kid, like
that; but he had that sort of a silly, sweet sound to his
laughter, the same as he had in his cussing, and I liked
to hear it.

"All right, señor," says Pepillo, "and what else will
you do for me?"

"Teach you manners," says I.

"How?" says he.

"This way," says I, and I make a pass at him. I grabbed thin air. He was just a mite faster moving than the lash of a four-horse whip when it curls over to snap the haunch of the near leader.

"You would beat me?" says Pepillo, dropping his head a little on one side and looking thoughtful.

"I would give you such a licking as nobody else could ever improve on," says I, "if I had the running of you, youngster!"

"So!" says Pepillo. "I am to be beaten and taught manners, and sent to school, maybe. And what else will you do?"

It appealed to something serious in me and I said: "Look here, kid, I'll tell you what I'll do. I'll start in and make a change in you. I'll keep you dressed clean and decent. I'll see that you have enough to eat. I'll see that nothing too much is ever asked of you. And besides that, I'll see to it that you get some of the bad ideas out of your head. I'll see that you turn straight. You got the makings of a damned little good for nothing thief, and d'you know what comes of thieves and such like, kid?"

"Ah," says Pepillo, making his eyes as big as moons, "tell me!"

"They die with a rope around their throats," says I.

"So!" gasps Pepillo. "Ah, señor!"

"You little devil," says I, "you're laughing at me, ain't you? But I tell you: what you need is a master, and I'll be one to you. I've been through hell myself, kid, and I know how to keep you from having to go through the same thing. You hear me talk?"

Pepillo leaned up against the side of the store, thinking very dark. He looked up to me, once or twice, with a smile in his eyes and on his lips, as if he was thinking what an awful lark it would be, and what an awful fool he would make out of me. Then he says:

"You might beat me, señor. You might take a very cruel whip and beat me with it until the blood ran down through my clothes, but if you laid a hand on me, señor, I should stab you to the heart!"

He looked like he meant it, too. He looked about as meek and submissive as a young loafer wolf.

"All right" says I. "I'll treat you like your name was Taliaferro. But if you join up with me, you got to promise that you'll stick to your side of the contract for a whole year. Y'understand? Before I'll blow in the price of a suit of clothes and all the rest on you."

"You shall have my hand on it!" says he.

I reached out and flicked a forefinger under his throat, and sure enough, I got hold of a silk string and jerked out a little ebony cross worked with fine gold and even set with jewels.

"Damn this hand shaking!" says I. "You're a Catholic, and you'll swear by the cross that you wear around your neck, youngster!"

He had clapped both hands over the cross and turned red and then pale. He was all worked up.

"You dog—you son of a dog—you bull-faced, big-jawed, stupid-eyed—"

"Go on," says I, "and when you get tired, let me know when you will talk sense again."

Well, he was a queer kid. All at once he stood up straight and he said "what shall I swear to you, señor, and what is your name?"

"Kitchin is my name," says I. "Which mostly they call me Blondy, you know."

"That's not a name," says this kid.

"My real name is a joke," says I.

"I cannot swear to a false name," says he, very seriously.

"It would spoil my time on the range if it was knowed," says I. "But as a matter of fact my front name is really Percival! That's a hot one, ain't it!"

"Then what am I to swear to you, Don Percival?" says he.

"To stick by me for a year and to do what you're told all that time."

"And you, señor?"

"I'll give you my word that I'll treat you fair and square, on my word of honor."

"You will not swear, then?"

"Not me, kid. I ain't struck any need of having any God in my rambles around this little old world. The nearest I've come to the power of God was twenty gents done up in blue coats and brass buttons, and wearing clubs—but they wasn't nothing to swear by."

Pepillo nodded: "Your word of honor is good enough for me," says he. He was tremendous serious as he went on: "I am a very bad boy, señor. I have done much wrong in my life. And if you can make me into a good man—"

Even in spite of his seriousness there was something about that that made him bust out laughing. When he sobered up, he grabbed hold on his cross and he tilted his head up to the sky, and he says, soft and shaky:

"I shall work for you and serve you in all things, so help me God!"

And he looked down slowly towards the earth again and stood there a while, thinking.

"Hey, Pepillo," says I, "smile, will you?"

"Ah, Señor Kitchin," says he, "it is a serious thing. It is a year out of my life, but I give it into your hands because I know that you will take care of me!"

He walked into the store to get fitted out by Gregorio, and I tried to figure out whether I liked him best sassy or serious, but I couldn't—except that when he was serious there was something about him that sort of scared me.

But in another minute I could hear him chirping in the store as gay as ever, and swearing at Gregorio, and beating the prices down. And that was a relief, I can tell you!

CHAPTER VII

That was in the days before every hired man had a Ford.
Automobiles was something to dream about, but not to
see. When I got to the brick hotel back in the white
man's part of Sour City, with Pepillo and my luggage in
the wagon, there was Randal setting up on the seat of a
buckboard reining in a pair of fine hosses and gentling
them down a little with his voice, because they was the
kind that needed gentling.

You could tell by one look at them hosses why it was
that Randal wasn't apt to make any howling success as
an economical rancher, because that span was a pair of
high-steppers that would of been more useful on a race
track than in toting hired men and their blanket rolls
back and forth to the ranch house, and bringing in
empty boxes and bringing out groceries and meat.

I threw in my luggage and climbed into the place
beside Randal, which was a pretty hard job, because
those hosses were all the time starting and backing and
starting up again and half-rearing, and prancing and
dancing and foaming and looking mighty pretty and useless, you can bet. But when I was settled, the kid jumped
into the back of the buckboard as slick as you please.

"What's this?" says Randal.

"That's my mozo," says I.

He give me a quick side glance.

"Whole hog, eh?" says he.

"Or none," says I.

"All right," says Randal. "I wish you luck, but I don't
think that you'll ever get by with the boys if you have
a servant like this. They ain't the kind that like servants."

"They'll like Pepillo," says I. "They'll like him, or be damned, and I don't think that I care much which."

You see, I was happy about that boy. He had a way with him that meant a good deal to me. He was sassy and he was a crook, but so was I. And I figgered that I could do a whole lot of good for him, and that he could do a whole lot of good for me, which is the best way to have any deal arranged—something on both sides, you know! But still, it rather tickled me to think that here was I, a jail-bird, aiming to take care of the raising of a kid like Pepillo that might of bothered a whole chapter of father confessors to look after him and his sins.

The road that we followed pitched up a pretty steep grade from Sour City and pretty soon we come to a height on a place where the road dropped over the top of a hill, and there Randal pulled up the hosses and nodded to me. I knew what he meant, and so I took a look, because I figured that this must be the ranch.

Starting from the outside, I circled my eye around on tall mountains, west and south and east, and where we was, towards the north, there was rolling hills, with a cut through them where Sour Creek rolled through on its way down the bigger valley outside. But inside those mountains and those hills there was as neat a valley as I ever hope to see, all checked about and crossed over with the little streams that run down to the Sour Creek. The sides of them streams was lined with trees. Also, there was groves dotted around casual, here and there, where the cows could lie down for shade in the middle of the day or get shelter in a storm, and where your eye could rest pretty pleasant.

I never seen a range where a gent could ride over with more pleasure than that Sour Creek valley. Right about in the middle, with the road pointing a straight white finger at it, there was the roof of a house, just about covered up with trees, at that distance, and I didn't have to ask that that was the ranch-house.

All I could do was to say: "Is the whole thing one ranch?"

Randal, he grinned sideways at me, that way that he had, and he nodded.

"The fences for the boundaries," says he, "run all around this here valley on the water divides. Uncle

Stephen picked out this place at a time when he could of fenced in the entire lower valley as well as this place, but he decided that this was enough for any one man to give his attention to work properly. So he settled down here. The old fool! He might have had ten millions in land if he'd spread himself a little more!"

I looked around and I didn't say nothing, but I'll tell you that I agreed with old Stephen and not with his nephew. Because that big oblong valley was a whopping piece of land. It would make your head ache if you was to close your eyes of a night and try to think of all the nooks and the corners on it and all of the landmarks. It just filled a man's eye, and it would certainly fill his hands, too. I didn't wonder that Uncle Stephen had been able to make fifty thousand dollars a year out of that land. I only wondered that he hadn't been able to make two hundred thousand out of it; or even more!

But that was before I had a chance to look close at the southern mountains. When I saw them close up, then I understood. Off at a little distance, they looked perfectly natural and nice and harmless, with some white streaks down the sides of them, but when you come closer, you could see that those streaks developed into a regular network across the faces of the mountains, and when you come closer still, you could see that every cord and crevice of that network was made by the work of the water that was flowing along through limestone formations and that had been working a few billions of years chawing out the stone and making itself white-walled cañons.

You talk about a labyrinth—that was it! I didn't have a chance to look at it close, of course, but before we got to the ranch-house, I could see there was about a thousand blind alleys among those mountains, and besides them, there was about a thousand alleys that wasn't blind. And maybe there was ways of making blind alleys into alleys that had a let-out in them. Take it by and large, a gent could walk every day of his life in those limestone alleys and try to get the plan of them into his head, but he never would of succeeded. Not a chance! What they needed was a gent with a brain that would understand everything that it seen at a glance and keep it printed solid in his head. You understand?

Randal, he got sort of nervous as we pulled along towards the ranch.

"You don't seem none too cheerful!" says he.

"Well," says I, "I've heard folks talk about a thieves' paradise, but till I seen those cañons, I didn't know what they meant, you see? Now I understand. Will you tell me, in the first place, just what sort of a gent that Uncle Stephen of yours was?"

"I'll show you pretty soon," says Randal.

We drove along about another mile up the valley and pretty soon he pulled up the hosses and pointed to a fence where the three lines of barbed wire lay hangin' on the ground and rusting themselves to death.

"About two days before Uncle Stephen died," says Randal, "he was riding along this way, and he wanted to see how his shooting eye was. And so he outs with his Colt and he blazes away with it in rapid succession three times, and when he got done with his shooting, there were the three wires hanging limp on the ground. The boys that were along with him thought so much of that bit of shooting that when Uncle Stephen died, a couple of days later, they swore that that fence should never be repaired, and they keep to their oath. Because of it, I have to let a fifty-acre field lie idle, as you see. But tradition is a great thing on this ranch, and I can't break the traditions. That broken fence stands for the ghost of Uncle Stephen, as you might say, and the boys won't have it fixed. But I wanted to show it to you to let you understand the sort of stuff that he was made of!"

It was enough. I looked at those three clipped wires and I understood!

You've heard what I think of revolvers for accuracy; and I don't stand alone. If you doubt me, you meet up with the head of the police department in a big town, and you talk to him. Maybe he's got under him a thousand men that are paid to carry revolvers and to practice with them. They get extra pay and prizes and a lot of glory for being able to shoot straight. They get ammunition furnished to them free for practice, and besides all that, they all know that it's in their own interest to know how to shoot straighter than the crooks. But you ask the chief if he's got three real revolver shots in his thousand men, and if he's an honest chief, he'll lose no time, but tell you that he ain't.

Well, when I seen the three clipped wires of that fence, I can't tell you how my arm ached and how my trigger finger went numb to think of all the hours and hours that Stephen Randal must of practiced to be able to shoot like that! It takes a gent that's a hero to have as much patience as that. And while he kept up his shooting, he ran a big ranch and chased thieves and kept his accounts, and made fifty thousand dollars a year, clear cash profit!

I didn't need no oil painting of Stephen Randal after that. I seen him just as clear as though I had had his cold eyes looking at me down the barrel of a gun. I seen him just as clear as though I had hit him with all my might and just busted my hand all to pieces on the edge of his jaw.

Says I to Randal: "All I got to do is to follow the example of a gent like that uncle of yours. All that I got to do is to step right inside of his boots, eh?"

Randal nodded. "It's about the only way that you could manage it, I guess," says he. "Uncle Stephen was a sort of a hero, around here. They all still talk about him. They take off their hats to him, and they take them off to nothing else in the world."

It looked pretty clear to me, and so I says: "Well, Randal, I'll tell you right now that this job is a bad one and there's about one chance in a hundred that it won't lick me. But I'll try my best. And here's where I start right in studying Uncle Stephen!"

CHAPTER VIII

Randal thought that there was no other idea half so good as that. He said that he himself would have tried to do the imitation of his Uncle Stephen, but there was a couple of things in his way. In the first place, Stephen Randal was a great big man, pretty near as big as me. In the second place, the sergeant was no sort of a hand with horses, and that was pretty near a fatal blow to anybody that would want to step into the real boots of his uncle, who couldn't get himself throwed by anything but an outlaw. He loved bucking horses so damn much that he wouldn't have quiet ones on his place!

I could handle hosses, and I was big and strong. Of course I was no hand with guns, but I had to hope that things would never come to a point where guns would be necessary. If a gent is steady enough and got nerve enough, guns *ain't* necessary. It's the weak fellow that feels ground slipping beneath him that has got to shoot.

When we drove up to the house, a nigger boy come out and took the heads of the hosses, and another unloaded the baggage.

Inside of the house, we could hear a reglar old high jinx going on. There was a piano banging somewhere in the offing, and half a dozen of the boys must of been doing a jig in lumbermen's boots, and the rest of them was whooping to help things along.

"Moonshine again," says Randal, and gives a sigh.

"Wait a minute," says I. "Is somebody died? Is that a wake, maybe?"

He explained that things was usually pretty noisy around the house at night. He said that during the time of his Uncle Stephen, he always let the men come in from the bunkhouse and use the big library and maybe the back living-room, if they wanted to. Except, of course, when he was giving a party, y'understand.

But when Harry Randal got into control, the men begun to spread. First they got into the habit of walking into the house through the front door, and then they got into the habit of hanging up their hats in the hall, and then they made the whole first floor of the house sort of into their quarters. What was worse, they began to bring in moonshine whiskey, and after the day's work, they would warm up and have a little fun of their own.

"Hell, Randal," says I, "why didn't you tell me this a long time ago?"

"I should of," he admitted, "but I was afraid to, old timer, for fear that you would back down on me. This is a hard nut to crack, and I know it. They're running wilder and wilder every minute of every day, and I've lost all control! And they make a fool of every ranch-manager that I bring out to the place. I can't fire them. It would simply be turning them into that many rustlers. Then they asked me to hire some puncher who was able to play the piano. I couldn't find one, and they went and found one themselves. He's a hardboiled one, too. His name is Rusty McArdle. He's a fellow who had a decent start but couldn't use it. His folks gave him an education, and he can play the piano; very well, as you can hear for yourself. Nature gave him a pair of shoulders just as broad as yours, but he let his education go to pot and he finally had to use his broad shoulders to make a living. He was too lazy to work and so he became a prizefighter and would have made himself a near-champion if it hadn't been that he made the town too hot to hold him. So he wound up on the range, and now he's landed here. Rusty McArdle will be your worst problem, Blondy!"

I listened to that riot in the house and thought about what Randal had said to me, and the more I thought the nearer I was to turning around and starting on back for the town. But I couldn't quit before I tried my hand.

I cleared my throat and asked Randal how his uncle was in the habit of meeting his men.

"He had a very breezy way," said Randal. "He would

walk in and smile at everybody and shake hands all round—"

That wasn't very easy for me. I'm no joy-bird, and smiling is my hardest job. But I decided that I would try that way of meeting this gang of thugs that called themselves cow-punchers.

I was all nerved up to this, and as we walked up to the door, Randal laid his hand on the knob.

"Are you ready?" said he, like he was going to introduce me on a stage.

"I'm ready," says I, feeling very shaky. "Let her go!"

Just then that Pepillo give my arm a tug.

"Señor," said he, "go straight to your room! Do not stop to talk with them!"

I give him one look, but his face was in the shadow. However, I knew that he must of heard our talk, and he must of got an idea that was working on the insides of him, and then the door opened. It let a blast of light out onto me, and I stepped into the house behind Randal and found myself in a reglar whirl of cigarette smoke.

Around that room was about a dozen or so of the toughest eggs that I ever laid eyes on. They was hand-picked. I'd been in Fulsom, not so long before, where I'd seen a choice lot of thugs and second-timers, but Fulsom's was a beauty gallery compared to that lot. I tell you hard they was. They wore their guns in the house!

I seen a sort of a smear and a blur of faces, but nothing more than general impressions right and left because everything was pulled to a focus on one man, and that was Rusty McArdle. He had got up from the piano stool and now he walked to the middle of the room. He was as big as me and made a lot better. Not so much hands and feet, but thicker through the chest and made tapering like a mast, other end up. He had a shock of hair the color of rust that had give him his name, and he had a pair of blue eyes that was filled to the brim with lightnings.

I never seen a gent like that, so filled with energy. It made you want to smile, just to see him. He could of walked out onto a stage and looked at the audience and just walked off again, and they would of clapped for him to come back! That's how much of a man he was.

But I wasn't in the audience. I was up there on the

stage with him, and I tell you what, it was an uncertain sort of a feeling. I would of been glad to be almost any other place rather than there.

"Well, boys," sings out Randal, "I've brought out a new man to run the place, and a good one. I hope that you'll all get on with him."

He had started out very brave and cheerful, but his voice wobbled like he was half choked before he got to the end. It was a miserable sort of a situation.

Not one of them devils said nothing. They just looked. Except Rusty McArdle, and he grinned straight in my face—the sort of a smile that says a lot more than words.

Right then I knew that there was no use staying in that room. I couldn't go around with a smile and shake hands with them all, after the style of the dead man. The kid had been right when he told me to go straight to my room.

"I'm going upstairs to get washed up," says I to Randal.

He sent a sick look at me, as much as to say: "This is a pretty lame beginning for you!" And then he led the way out of that big living-room, and the dimness of the hall outside was like a blessing on my eyes, I can tell you.

Randal didn't say anything till he got me upstairs, where he showed me into a fine big room with a double bed in it, and curtains at the windows, and a carpet on the floor, and everything extreme civilized. There he began to pace up and down.

"Why didn't you say something?" said Randal. "Why didn't you strike while the iron was hot? You sneaked away like a beaten cur! My God, Blondy, you've ruined things before you even had a chance to put them right. You might as well start back for town, now, but if I were you, I'd climb out a window. I wouldn't go back through that room to the front door!"

I wouldn't ordinarily take talk like that from any man, no matter what money he was paying to me, but just then my spirit was a mite broke.

"Listen!" says he. "That's for you."

From downstairs, there come a roar of laughter, and I knew that Randal was right. That was for the new manager of the ranch!

Then from the corner of my eye I seen that Pepillo

nodding towards Randal and hooking his thumb over his shoulder towards the door. I took that hint.

"Leave me be for a while, Randal," says I. "I want to be alone and think this thing over. You're not helping me any. Things are about as bad as they can be, out here, and you're not helping any!"

He had a lot more to say, and I could see the bad look in his eye that means that a gent has his steam away up high. But it seemed to occur to him that maybe there was still a ghost of a chance that I could turn some sort of a trick for him and for myself. So he left everything else unsaid and flung out of the door, and slammed the door behind him.

I listened to the echo of it crashing from wall to wall, and I was sicker than ever. My courage was about down to zero. As far as that rough gang downstairs was concerned, I could see myself as one of them, but I could never see myself handling those tough fellows with a bad one like Rusty McArdle at the head of them to tell them what to think.

Pepillo woke me up a little. He shied his hat into a corner of the room and made a face at the door.

"That," said he, "is a pig, is it not?"

I couldn't help grinning, in spite of my misery.

"No," said I, "he ain't a pig. He's a fur-bearing animal that's smaller than a pig and has a lot worse smell. That's what he is. Now what's inside of your head?"

He sat down on the table and folded his legs in under him very neat; and there he sat with his chin on his two small fists grinning at me.

CHAPTER IX

Just to look at him was enough to cheer a man up a good deal. For instance, have you ever seen a blue jay fluttering around through the trees? You know that the murderer and thief and gossip is going around hunting for trouble and ready to talk even where they ain't anything to make talk about, but still, there is something so bright about a jay when the sun hits him, and he looks so sassy and so happy that you can't help smiling.

It was that way with Pepillo. He was a mischief-maker, and there wasn't any doubt about that, but you couldn't help smiling in spite of the damage that he might be doing. Right then, I couldn't tell whether he was laughing with me or at me, but it didn't make a whole lot of difference.

I should tell you how he had fixed himself up in the store. He had wrangled Gregorio out of a pair of red morocco boots that you could see a mile away, they was so shining, and always looked as though he had just waded across a pool of blood. And he had a tan-colored linen suit on him, with a sort of an underjacket of a very bright green-blue. He had a yellow shirt, and a black felt hat with a red feather stuck in one side of it. He looked like something out of a book—and an old-time book, at that! A queer set of clothes, that was. It sort of took my breath, the first time that I seen them on him, but he had a way about him that just set off those clothes. He was as fierce as a hawk, and as graceful as a swallow. He was like a cross between a singing bird and a falcon. I feasted my eyes on him and he grinned at me, and all the time the lights in his eyes kept changing, as the fires inside of his

50

devilish little head kept burning mean or kind. I didn't know whether he was gunna sympathize with me, or mock me, or give me good advice.

He says: "The pig—this what you call him, fur-bearing animal—this Randal, he does not count, no-o-o-o?"

He had a way of saying the word like that, letting his voice go half an octave up the scale while he hung unto his question-mark.

"Maybe he don't, but that leaves plenty more of the rest that *do* count!"

He only shook his head, Pepillo did. He jumped down from the table and went into the corner of the room. He picked up his hat and flaunted out the crimson feather on it, and he stuck it on his head and gave the hat a cock onto one side.

Then he rolled himself a cigarette. It was a treat to watch him, making his little nimble fingers go faster than your eye could follow, and doing it all with one hand, while he looked at you and talked about something else. He was terrible proud of the way that he could roll a cigarette. He lighted his smoke and blew out a puff at the ceiling.

"There is only one!" says Pepillo.

"Only one what?" says I.

"Ha! señor!" says he. "If I am to do your thinking for you, you must follow me closely."

"You damn little blue-jay," says I, "how can I listen to what you got to say when I'm so busy watching you?"

"Is it so?" says Pepillo.

He takes a step or two so's he can view himself in the mirror at the other end of that room. There he stands, cocking his head a little to one side and then a little to the other. Then he makes a bow and gives a smile to the image of himself in the mirror.

"It is true," says Pepillo. "I am worth looking at. And shall I not have success when I grow up?"

It wasn't hard to guess that what he meant was success with the ladies, and, of course, he was right. With that silver voice and that wonderful pair of eyes and handsome face, he would be sure to grow up into a regular heartbuster.

"Ah," says I to Pepillo, "if you live out the next two or three years, you'll be leaving me to marry a girl."

"Do not fear, señor," says Pepillo. "For, when I leave

you to marry the beautiful American heiress, I shall take you with me!"

"What might I be doing then?" says I.

"You would be my valet, señor."

There was nothing handy but my quirt, and he dodged that. He could almost of dodged a bullet, he was so lightning fast with his feet.

"However," says I, "you ain't gunna live that long, because I'm gunna get so mad at you, some day, that I'll put out a hand—"

"And grasp a nettle, señor," says the blue jay.

You couldn't put him down. It was like hitting a cork in the water.

"But," goes on Pepillo, "this Randal is no help and he is no hindrance. As for the rest, they might each of them be dangerous, except that there is one of them so much greater than the rest."

"You mean that Rusty McArdle?" says I. "Yes, and a lot too dangerous for me, I guess!"

"Bah!" yelled Pepillo, and stamped his red boot. "Are you not ashamed to confess such a fear to me?"

"You're my conscience, kid," says I. "You're my bad conscience, and I don't mind you seeing the shadier side of me. Yep, I'm afraid of that McArdle."

"So?" says the kid—and he smiled at me. But there wasn't any mirth in that smile. It was one of the kind that show all the teeth and makes a man look like a cat—plumb mean. They have a way of smiling like that down in Mexico. "You are afraid, then. But why?"

"Why?" says I. "You had a look at him, didn't you?"

"I had a dozen looks," says he.

I believed it, too. Those dark brown eyes of his was about twelve times as fast as the eyes of anybody else.

"And what did you see?" says I.

"A big man," says he.

"A *damn* big man."

"He does not work," said Pepillo. "So he cannot be as strong as he looks."

"Some need hard work to keep their muscles up," said I, "and some are born strong and stay strong. This Rusty is one of that kind."

Said Pepillo: "You are beaten before you strike a blow!"

"There wouldn't be many blows," said I. "That Rusty

wears a gun, and he's got a nervous sort of a hand. He can shoot, fast and straight, and don't you have any doubts about it."

"So can you, señor. Did I not see you pick out a revolver that meant much business?"

"You saw me pick out a bluff," I answered. "If the boys out here ever see my gun—while I'm cleaning it, say —I want them to see a gat that looks real mean. But it's all a bluff. I can't shoot for sour grapes."

"A bluffer, too!" snarled Pepillo. "What kind of a man are you, señor?"

"Enough of a man to turn you upside down and shake the coin out of your pockets!" said I.

I thought that that would make him mad, but it didn't. He just nodded.

"True!" said Pepillo. "Of a hundred, you were the only one to see through me. That is very important, because it is not easy to look through me. Not at all!"

Sure of himself? That's putting it mildly. I never saw such a case of fat-head in my life. But it wasn't very offensive. I don't know why.

"With this Rusty, the fight would be with guns," I finished up.

"You are wrong," said Pepillo. "He would fight in any way that you want. He has never been beaten, and therefore, he would fight with the hands; and you have much hands, señor!"

"His hands may be smaller, but they're just as mucher a mine. You see, you ain't got a move left, youngster!"

He flicked his cigarette into a corner and let it burn its way into the carpet; the little rapscallion! Then he took out a pair of slim yellow gloves and says: "I don't know. I have never been beaten in a place where I had plenty of time."

"There's no time here," said I. "Right now to-night is when I got to do something!"

"Time?" says this kid. "Five minutes is a long time! Wait, and you shall see. But I must have quiet, if I'm to think!"

And he looked down to the floor and frowned. Up from below come a regular roar of shouting and laughter. The boys down there were taking another pass at the moonshine and livening themselves up for some sort of deviltry that they might have in mind. It give me a shivver because I didn't have to think twice to guess that what they meant was something connected with the new manager on the ranch.

Pepillo started to turn around, but while he was doing that, he got another flash of himself in the mirror and paused to enjoy himself, standing like that, just poised on one foot like a dancer, and drawing his gloves very slow and easy through his hand.

"Ah, well," says Pepillo, "I shall have to go down and speak to them myself, if you will not!"

"Hey," says I, "wait a minute, kid. If you go down there, they'll take you apart to see what makes you tick! You don't know these roughs!"

"So?" says this little cocky blue jay. "But I tell you, that in the part of the country where I was raised, these rough men would not be rough enough to be more than house mozos! No more than that!"

And he flicked the door open and slipped away into the hall outside.

CHAPTER X

The minute that Pepillo was gone, I was ate up with curiosity to see what he would really do, if he actually dared to go right into the room where those cowpunchers and Rusty McArdle were having their high-jinx.

I couldn't very well follow him down the stairs and so look through the open doorway, so I did what Randal had suggested to me a little earlier. I heaved myself through the open window and climbed down the side of the house. It was only a story to go down, and there was a drain from the gutter at the eaves of the roof, that ran down the wall beside my window. The grip in my hands was always my strongest point, and so I was able to lower myself to the ground dead easy.

I found myself right up against the back windows of the big living-room, and when I peeked through, I could see the whole layout.

Rusty had a glass of red-eye in one hand and he was making a little speech with the other, as you might say. That speech must have been something about me, by the way that he pointed and looked above him, now and then, and by the way that the boys all roared with laughter, I could guess that he was arranging something extra special for me.

However, by the time that I got to an open window, where I could hear everything just as well as I could see it, he had finished his speech. Then the door opened and somebody says: "There comes his mozo!"

"The little rat looks like he was pretty sure of himself," says another.

He did, too. You would think that Pepillo had come

55

down from the king of England to tell the stable boys that they was acting real bad. He makes a couple of steps into the room and stands there and looks around him, and gives a flash of those bright eyes of his to every face. He got his silence, too. I suppose that maybe it was wonder at the nerve of that little kid, and maybe it was because they was curious to hear what he would say.

He says: "Amigos, it is not unknown to you that my master is now yours."

They fair blinked when he shot that home at them. Then one of them roared: "Why, damn my heart, they don't make the kind of men that can be master to gents like us. You hear us kid?"

"You've had your thought for this month, Shorty," says Rusty McArdle.

This Shorty, that had answered up, was one of the queerest made men that ever stepped into stirrups. He wasn't more than five feet high, and about three and a half of those feet must have been his body. His legs was hardly long enough to bother about, and they was bowed out to fit the side of a horse. He was near as broad as he was long, and when he was sitting down in a chair, his hanging hands just about touched the floor. Like an ape, you'd say. Not that he had the monkey look, though, because he looked too mean to be stupid. A real stupid gent never looks like poison, and that was what Shorty would remind you of.

Pepillo, he just put up his hand to command silence, when they all growled at him.

"I don't mind telling you," said he, "that I've had to persuade the señor from coming down here to you. It was a hard task, but I was able to do it, and I have come myself to tell you that it will be wiser for you to keep quiet, here!"

It brought a fair howl from those wild men, and it brought a cold sweat out on me. It looked as though Pepillo was sort of inspired. He couldn't of said wronger things if he had studied for a year. I think that one or two of them would of got out and made a rush for the kid, right then and there, but Rusty McArdle, he waved them back.

"This is sort of amusin'," says he to the kid. "Your boss, he must be a sort of a duke, or something?"

"That," says Pepillo, as quick as a wink, "is something that you had ought to ask his gun!"

"Oh," says Rusty. "By the way that he come in and went out of the room again, to-night, we all sort of suspected that he might of left his gun behind him!"

It brought another roar from the boys. They liked the way that Rusty phrased things for them. And it *was* pretty neat, you got to admit.

However, it didn't bother the Blue Jay. He tilted up his head a little and he slapped his gloves into his other hand, as pert as you please.

"I shall tell you something for your good," says the kid. "The señor has a most frightful temper. Even I am sometimes afraid of him—"

He made a pause there, as though he expected them to laugh. And they did; they pretty near busted themselves.

"Leave him be, boys," says Rusty. "I want to hear all the rest of this. I guess that four-flusher upstairs has taught him this spiel by heart before he come down. Go on, little one!"

"Ah, friend," said the Blue Jay to Rusty, "I am too kind to repeat to him everything that you have said. I do not wish to see you die!"

That seemed to tickle the boys a lot. Hard as they was, it was easy to see that they looked on Rusty as about the hardest thing this side of chilled steel—and I felt the same way about him. All that I wanted was to wring the kid's neck. And then my second idea was that I had better get ready to hop onto a horse and ride for Sour City as fast as four strong legs and a pair of spurs would take me. However, I waited out this talk, half trembling and half dying out of curiosity to know what that little thickheaded, sassy devil would have the nerve to say next to the lions. But you never would of guessed.

"I like your sympathy," says Rusty. "I ain't ambitious to fill no early grave. I've dodged it a couple of times, so far, and somehow, I don't see anything in your boss to make me worry."

Pepillo looked him over and up and down, so long and so steady that finally it made even Rusty stop grinning and begin to frown.

"What are you looking at, youngster?" says he.

"I am only wondering," says the Blue Jay, "how the señor will kill you!"

Pretty sassy, that, but Rusty come right back.

"With help," says he. "He'll never manage it by himself!"

"I do not think it will be with a gun," says the kid.

"I don't think so either," says Rusty; and the gang yelled with their pleasure, again.

"It will be with his hands," says the kid, "because there is enough of you to entertain him for a few moments. However, if you have sense enough to come to your wits now, and if you will ask my pardon, señor, and then beg me to intercede for you with the señor, I may be able to get you off."

"Hell, boy," says Rusty McArdle, "I'm doggoned if you don't sort of rile me. Now you trot right on back to your boss, and you tell him that this sort of a bluff was pretty good fifty years ago, but that the world has growed up, since, and that the most growed up part of the world is the gents that is sitting in this room right now, and looking you in the face!"

They all had to rumble their pleasure, at that. Nothing that pleases a man so much as being considered mighty dangerous.

"After all," says Pepillo, "I suppose that it is better to have it over with at once. I shall tell him what I have heard."

He turned around on his heel, as cool as ever. But then Shorty started up out of his chair and come along across the floor with an ugly waddle of a step.

"Wait a minute, grasshopper," says Shorty. "You tell him extra-special from me, that he don't need to start in with Rusty McArdle. Rusty is a man-sized man. But me, I'm the kid, around this ranch. And still, I'm plenty good enough to make that bluffer take water and like it. You tell him that he'll have to start in with me, or else the boys won't waste no time on him. They'll just roll him in some spare tar that they got handy and then fix him up a coat of feathers. You tell him that!"

"Shall I tell him that—from dirt like you?" says Pepillo.

And while that word simply paralyzed all the nerves in the body of Shorty, and made his huge arms swing sort of helpless at his side, what did the kid do but waltz up and switch Shorty across the face with his gloves—flick-flack, just like that! It paralyzed me, too, when I seen it. And it wasn't with the fingers of the gloves; it was with the buckle ends of them, and one of the buckles tore Shorty's lip a little and sent a stream of blood trickling down towards his chin.

I had a chance to watch all of this, because Shorty was so dumb with rage and astonishment and humiliation that he simply couldn't move; and all the while Pepillo was turning around and walking off as easy and as slow as you please. He got to the door while the mad-bull look was still gathering on the face of Shorty.

But it exploded, just then. He gave a roar that didn't have any words in it. His eyes had turned red, and his mouth worked in, a horrible way to see. Then he lunged after the Blue Jay with both of his long, thick arms stretched out. And his hands, they was like the legs of pouncing spiders—hands bigger than mine, even!

That door flicked shut behind Pepillo, but not in any hurry. However, he must have locked it that instant when he was on the other side, because Shorty reached the door and smashed against it. But he recoiled without opening it.

"That kid needs a quirting down," says somebody with a yell. "And we'll take his boss along with him! Come on, boys!"

Ay, they were willing and ready for that sort of a game. Pepillo had just roused their bloods. Maybe, ordinarily, they would of had the good sense and the decency to admire the kid for his nerve and his sassy way, but I suppose that they'd had a little too much red-eye.

Most of all, there was a lot of them together, and maybe you notice that a mob always makes itself worse or better than any man in it. Either a mob is all angels or all devils, and it's easier to be all devils than it is to be all angels. However, a hundred men is always braver than any one man; and a hundred men is always stupider and more cowardly than any one man.

This night, the punchers on the Randal ranch was in a bad way and they meant trouble, big trouble, and stacks of it, long continued. I seen them rush that door and pile up against it, but it was made of strong stuff and they couldn't open it, just yet. I took one more glimpse of their faces, for they was plain slavvering with rage, then I turned away.

I wanted to get clean of that place and hike for Sour City. I never wanted anything so bad in all my born days.

I never was a hero. I don't pretend to be a hero. A good mix and a free-for-all—sure, that is fun and good fun; but those twelve men meant murder!

However, I thought about the kid in the nick of time. No matter what a mess he had made of things, he no doubt had meant right, and if those ruffians got hold of him, they would near kill him.

I went up that drainage pipe faster than I ever went any place in my life. I fair ran with my hands.

When I come to the window of my room, I looked in, and there was Pepillo with all of the sap run out of him. He was sitting at the table, with his head bowed in his arms, sobbing like a baby!

CHAPTER XI

It hit me bad. You wouldn't believe how mighty awful bad it did hit me. I've seen growed up men, strong and all that, get hurt so bad, that they cried—and there's nothing much worse than that—but somehow this kid had seemed more stronger than any man. There was so much sap in him, so much sassiness, and meanness, and go to him, that I couldn't imagine him breaking down; not if there was a whole battery of guns turned loose and looking him right in the eye.

However, there he was, sitting with his head down, and his whole skinny little body shaking with sobs. It flabbergasted me. I called from the window! "Kid, it's time to go!"

He leaped from that table as though a bullet had gone through him: a bullet of joy, I should say, because all at once he was smiling through the tears. He give two flicks with his hands to his face, and every last one of those tears was gone galley-west, and only a sparkle of them left in his long, black lashes.

"I thought you had gone!" gasps the Blue Jay. "I thought that you had sneaked down—and that you were afraid—and that you had run away from me!"

"I *did* sneak down," says I; "and I did see; and I *was* afraid; and I'm thinkin' of leavin' you here flat and cold, unless you hurry up and come along with me!"

Downstairs, there was the yelling and the yapping of those crazy fighting men; and the kid, he just rested his hands against the edge of that table, and he says to me, smiling:

"I feared that you had gone away from me. I feared

61

that you had run away and thought only of yourself. Oh, señor!"

Yes, sir, you would of thought that I was Santa Claus, to see his blush and his silly grin. Or that I was his best girl come back to him after a long parting.

"You damn rattle-brains," says I, "don't you hear them yelling? They'll be up here in a minute. Yes, I've seen and I've heard you, and of all the fool jobs that I ever seen in the world, you done the most foolish and the worst in every way. You've pretty near dug a grave for me here in this house. Now you come tearing, or I'll start along without you!"

Damn my eyes, he didn't budge! No, sir, he just stood there, and he smiled at me, perfectly contented and happy.

"Hurry! I got to start, Pepillo!" says I.

He just shakes his head: "Ah, no, señor, you will not leave me!"

I didn't know what could be working in his head, the young fool! I started down the pipe, calling: "All right, here I go!" But I didn't hear him coming with a rush to the window, and so I heaved myself back and looked in, and there he was, standing right by the table and smiling at the window, still.

"You see, it will not do. I understand!" That's what he says to me!

"You understand what, you blockhead? You understand nothing," says I to him. "Why, you empty-skulled kid, they'll tear you to bits, if they lay hands on you. You understand?"

"They will not lay hands on me," says Pepillo, as easy as ever.

"Doggone me," I yelled at him, "you've gone nutty. You have, for a fact! I want to know what will keep them from getting their hands on you, then?"

"You, señor," says he, very sweet.

It made me so mad and it bewildered me so that I thought I would choke. I couldn't see. A mist come up before my eyes.

"I'd like to wring your idiot neck myself," says I, meaning every word. "Pepillo!"

No, he only shook his head and smiled still. I was sure that he was crazy, now.

"Pepillo," I begged him, "for God's sake come along, before you get the pair of us killed by staying here!"

He canted his head to one side, like a bird on a branch in the summer sunshine.

"I cannot go, señor. I have too much pleasure hearing the music of the pack!"

"By God!" says I. "Crazy or not, they won't spare you. And if you won't come willing, I'll take you by force!"

I heaved myself in through the window and I made a pass at him. Strike me dead if I didn't nearly get a knife jabbed through the palm of my hand.

There stands Pepillo in the corner of the room with that damned, Mexican, mean smile, showing all of his teeth at me. And there was one of his long, thin-bladed knives in his hand.

"If you touch me, I'll kill you, señor!" says he. "I have promised you that before, and now I swear it to you on my honor and on the cross that I wear!"

"You treacherous polecat!" says I.

But I was staggered and all abroad. I didn't know what to do or where to turn next. I never seen actions that looked more like insanity, and yet the Blue Jay was the last person in the world to go crazy. He was more apt to drive other folks mad!

He stands there and he changes his smile to a real one.

"It is very pleasant, señor. Feel how the house trembles as they break down the door? They will be here, and at once!"

Ay, at that moment, they sent down the lower door with a great smashing and crashing that went echoing through the house, and I heard a yell in a room near to mine. I knew the voice, and it was Randal's. I was glad, anyway, that he should have some of the misery that I was having. I only wished that he had it all, for bringing me out to a set of tigers like these crazy men.

However, that didn't get Pepillo any the nearer to the window; and I had only the split part of a second, now, to move him. Up the stairs I could hear their feet making thunder. I reached for the drawer of the table, first, and jerked it open to snatch out my gun.

By the Lord, it was gone. The drawer of the table was empty. And when I looked up, feeling pretty drawn and desperate, that rat of a boy showed me my Colt.

"If you try a gun, they will surely kill you, señor, and

for that reason I took the temptation away from you. You must fight them with your hands, señor!"

Yes, sir, I swear that that is what the Blue Jay stood up and said to me. And as calm as you please—a whole lot calmer than I am as I write this here down in black and white! I get wild all over again. He sure was calculated to try out the strength of a man's nerves, that Pepillo was!

I says: "Pepillo, you are most likely the death of me, but I'm gunna make one more try to save you from them devils. Will you come?"

"Be warned, señor," says he. "I shall not come—not I! Not a step from this room!"

"In the name of the sweet Lord, will you tell me why in hell you *won't* come?" I groaned at him.

"Ah, well," says Pepillo, "you would not understand."

"Talk out!" says I.

"It is because your honor is lost if you run away—and you will not run away if I stay here!"

There it was: the cat was out of the bag at last. No, this Blue Jay, he wasn't crazy. He was worse than crazy. He was what the chaplain had always used to call "romantic." Everything wild that the chaplain didn't like, he used to call it romantic. A pretty good word, that; which it means, got out of fool story-books.

All the bad criminals: "They aren't really bad," the chaplain used to say to me all of the time. "It's just that the romantic vein has run away with them, and they want to imitate the greatness of other criminals before them. All because the writers of idiotic romances have made the idea seem attractive. And that's all that there is to it!"

Good old chaplain! He mostly had an idea for everything, but in that spot maybe he was partly right. And certainly when I stood there helpless in front of that fool kid, I seen that he was right about what made the wheels go round in Pepillo.

Honor!

He didn't want me to run away from that house because I would lose my honor!

Maybe was I a knight, or a baron, or something?

Had the king give me a trust?

Honor!

And me that was fresh out of two years in a state penitentiary! Honor!

I yelled: "You peanut head! You little yap! Honor? I tell you that I'm just out of the state pen! D'you still talk about my honor?"

"Ah, señor," said he, "I trust you completely and utterly. You must stay for the sake of your great soul!"

"My great foot!" says I. And I made a dive at him.

Well, sir, he heaved himself up stiff and straight and raised the knife in the air, and there was such a white devil in his face and such cold steel in his eyes that I couldn't do the trick. All the nerve run out of me and I stood there panting and damning him. I was half exhausted. That minute of clashing my will against the will of that mite of a kid made me feel just as though that I had run a mile at full speed.

And then: "They have come for you, my master!" said the Blue Jay.

Wham! Crash! They reached the door of that room.

"Come out," I hear them yell. "We want the man-killer. We want the new boss. We want to have a look at him and see what's inside of him! Are you comin' out, boss?"

That was a whole chorus of them, but chiefly there was the bull-roar of that Shorty above all the rest of them. And when I listened to them I turned away from Pepillo, feeling mighty weak, I can just tell you!

"Señor," says the kid behind me. "Do not let them come in at you! If you do that, you are lost!"

"Why, you little unspeakable fool!" says I. "There's one man alone out there that's more than a match for me! There's Rusty. He's got everything that I have and something more!"

"It is a great lie!" says Pepillo. "He is not a bulldog, as you are! He is only a tiger—dreadful for one minute, and then very weak! You will see!"

"And the rest of the crowd?"

"They will be nothing!" said the kid. "Oh, if I had half of your strength, I would step out and throw them in a heap!"

He would of, too. There was that stuff in him that makes one man the boss over twenty—but there wasn't any of that kind of stuff in me, I can tell you!

However, I saw that it was better to die fighting than

it was to die standing still, and so I sashayed up to the door and turned around and I says to the kid: "Pepillo, you are a thousand kinds of a fool, but you're game, God bless you. So long, because I ain't apt to see you again!"

I said that, and he give me a smile and a wave of his hand. What surprised me was that he was white as a sheet, with the eyes just sticking out of his head. Exactly as though even Pepillo was scared, too, but didn't want me to see it. However, I didn't have any time to work that all out with my slow-motion mind.

I jerked that door open and I dived out at the crowd of them that was outside.

CHAPTER XII

Did you ever see a rat that was cornered by dogs? It flies in their faces. That was what I done. It wasn't courage. You don't call a rat brave.

But I was partly desperate and partly I was mad. I don't mean angry, but crazy. Just that! The idea that this mite of a kid had deliberately worked up a trap for me to try out my "honor"—why, it was enough to make me laugh all the rest of my days; me being a jail-bird, and the rest of it as I've told you before.

I seen a blur of faces, and I jumped at them. The boxing that I had been doing at Fulsom, it made my hands work instinctive. I felt my knuckles bite through flesh to the bone. A pair of them went down, yelling, and tangled up a couple more as they fell, bringing them down at the same time, and I waded along through that gap and found the snarling face of Shorty in front of me. He whaled away with a long arm swing that would of knocked a hole right through the ribs of an ox, but he was a mite too slow, and I was inside of the punch in time.

I took Shorty by his throat, and he dropped back and straight down the stairs, with me on top of him. We done one somersault complete down that flight of stairs and through the door into the living-room. When I picked myself up, there was no stir in Shorty. He had got his head whanged on the steps until he was done, complete. But I didn't have empty hands long. The whole tangle of the punchers was coming down those stairs with a rush and a roar, and of course the first man down was the fastest of the lot. He happened to be the biggest, too.

I mean Rusty McArdle, if you have to be told. As he

came through the doorway, he seen my empty hands, and he shied his Colt across the room. It exploded when it hit, and by luck, it sent a bullet humming an inch from my head, as if it was trying to fight for its boss even when it was out of his hand.

I seen that big chap come driving, and I let him have it. Oh, it was a pretty thing to see the way that he ducked under my wallop! I was the prettiest thing in the world, if you was off at a distance, watching. Natural speed, and ring training, that was what he had. He ducked under my punch, as I was saying, and coming up again, he clipped me with an uppercut right on the button.

Just like somebody had hit you on the back of the head with a hammer; that was the way it felt to me. It let loose a bomb that exploded inside of my head. My knees turned into worn-out springs, and they almost let me down to the floor. I did start falling, but I fell into McArdle as he tore in. He tried to tear himself loose, but I hung on for my life, and while he smashed at my ribs, my head cleared.

He fought himself away and bashed at me with a full arm punch, his teeth set, and his eyes full of the joy of fighting. Lord, Lord, but that was a punch! It ought to of tore the head off my shoulders, of course, but he was just a little too anxious to finish me then and there. He was "pressing," as the golf nuts call it, and the result was that he didn't hit the ball at all!

I was able to back out of the sweep of his fist, and as he lunged in, he tried to cover up, but he tried too late. I got him! It was a sweet feeling, I tell you. I got him on the chin with a lifting punch that snapped his head straight back onto his shoulders and flopped him on the floor as flat as a pancake.

What I wanted to do was to drop on top of him and choke him down, reglar rough and tumble, but my own head was filled with nightmares and cobwebs and dust. I couldn't exactly locate the place where he was lying on the floor, I was so groggy, and then I heard one of the cowpunchers saying, in a mighty respectful sort of a voice:

"Look at that, bunkies! This gent is giving Rusty a fair fight; and there's Rusty on the floor for the first time in his life!"

Ay, they seemed to be staggered by the look of things

as much as I was staggered by the fist of Rusty. Then my head cleared altogether, and I saw Rusty come up off the floor—bad hurt, by the wild look in his eye, and startled, too, as though he hadn't known that hands were made that could flatten him, this way, lucky punch or not!

He came tearing, and I set myself and let him have it as he plunged, one for each side of his head. It slowed him up, but it didn't stop him. He was a tiger. That part of what Pepillo had said was true enough. He got in close and then he began to hammer at me with the fastest flock of fists that I ever saw or heard of.

I tried to back away from that cloud of hornets, but it was like a bull trying to back away from a wildcat. The cowpunchers were going wild with joy, and their yelling seemed to take Rusty up on a wave top and throw him after me. I tried to dodge his rush, but it was a clumsy try, compared with his neat footwork. Just as I sidestepped, he slammed me. Everything turned to air under me, and I dropped a thousand feet and landed on bedrock.

I felt McArdle drop on top of me, and right then and there would of been the finish of Blondy Kitchin, because that fellow had his thumbs on my throat. Being knocked down had maddened him and he was ready for a kill. But this was no bar-room fight in Chicago. This was on the range, and these here were range-men that were watching. They got to him in a cluster, and through the blackness that was over my eyes, I seen them coming like shadows, and Shorty was the first of the lot. They grabbed Rusty McArdle and pulled him off me.

"Not that way, Rusty!" I heard them yell at him. "When he flattened you, he give you a chance to get up again!"

I heard Rusty say: "I forgot! I'm sorry I lost my head. Yes—he's a white man!"

"He'll never get up," says one of them. "He's got enough!"

I agreed with them, too. I had enough. I was beaten. My skull, it was just a copper bell, and there was hammers beating in it. But all at once a voice like a needle ran through my brain and stopped the hammers clattering and booming.

"Señor! Señor! In the name of God!"

Pepillo—he couldn't let me be! And that voice of his

was like a dash of cold water through my body. It braced me up, and raised me to my knee. I steadied myself there, with my head clear as a crystal, for the minute. I looked up at Big Rusty McArdle, and he nodded to me and says through his teeth:

"Step up, stranger! I want to get in one more pass at you! You're the first that ever come for a second one!"

I came, well enough, but I came low and managed to lunge in under the whip of his arm as he tried for my head. I came up in close, and sank my right fist with all of my weight behind it into his ribs. Seemed to me like my hand went in up to the wrist, and I heard a gasp and a groan from Rusty.

But he fought himself away quick as a wink. He was hurt, by the twisted look of his face. He was hurt, too, by the scared expression on the faces of the cowpunchers as they stood around and watched. But he wasn't too hurt to fight! He was nothing but game, that McArdle. He came at me—tiger, tiger, tiger all the time. He drove me before him. My head, it was simply rocking from one side to the other, but he was fighting too vicious to set himself well for a knockout, and as my shoulders hit the wall on the farther side of the room, I pitched forward, and managed to fall into another clinch.

I was sick, all right. Everything was a blur, except for a lightning flash that let in the sight of Pepillo on his knees, as though he had been praying, and the squeak of his voice as he yelled to me:

"Señor, señor! He weakens! The battle is yours!"

Why, numb and dumb as I was, that imp knew the way to shoot life into me. I got new strength in me. I grabbed McArdle harder, and it seemed to me that he sort of winced and buckled under my hand. Then I knew that he was going.

"Rusty," said I, "you're a tiger, but now you're done. Will you give up?"

He gasped at my ear: "I'll see you damned first! Stop clawing me and stand off and fight like a man, if you dare!"

I just laughed at him through the cloud that covered my eyes. I pushed him away, and he staggered back, with his knees sinking. Oh, condition was telling, now. He was strong; and he was fast as chain lightning, but he didn't have in his arms the seasoning of two years of hard labor.

It was Fulsom that was fighting for me now; just as much as the voice and the sight of the damned little imp, Pepillo.

Game, though; McArdle was game as steel. He tried to cover up his weakness by rushing, but he had spent himself in the rally that had driven me across the room. I stopped that rush with a half-arm left, and then I hit him away like a spinning top with a long right.

His knees were too weak to stop him. He kept reeling and staggering, and from the effects of that last punch, his head sagged from side to side.

I heard Shorty gasping: "Buck up, Rusty. For Gawd's sake, don't go down. It ain't possible! It ain't possible!"

It *was* possible, though. He was helpless, and all that I had to do was follow him up and hit him once more. But the effort to knock him out would probably set me staggering too, and I didn't want those fellows to see how nearly I was beaten.

I said: "Rusty, you're beat. I want you to take some time and come to. I'm going outside to wait till your head is cleared. This time it was fists; the next time it'll be guns. You get ready for the guns! Or else get ready to tell me that I'm the boss!"

And I started for the door, studying every step to keep from wobbling.

CHAPTER XIII

I got along through the doorway fine as silk and found myself safe out in the dark, with the night wind cooling off my face and the stars shining over me.

"I'm all right!" says I to myself. "All I got to do is to take a couple of deep breaths. Then my head will clear and I can figure out what I'll do if big Rusty decides to call my bluff. I can relax!"

Well, that was what I done. I relaxed. I loosened up my jaw muscles and I let go of myself all over. But when I say that I let myself go, I want you to know that it was exactly as though I was falling a whole block. A wave of darkness started up at me from the ground. The stars, they begun to spin around and turn into red globes, and the red globes exploded like shells, and each turned into a million rockets shooting across the night horizontal.

I didn't choose the place to fall. I just stretched myself out on the dry grass and wished for help.

It was that punch of Rusty's that had knocked me down. By rights, I had been about unconscious all this time if the voice of the kid hadn't jabbed a needle into me and braced me up in spite of myself. The rest of that fight was just nerves, as far as I was concerned. And now that I relaxed, I was down and out.

I heard a step and I figured that one of them had come out and now they would see what a bluffer I was, but I was too sick to care. Then the voice of Pepillo came dropping to me like rain on the desert. There was never nothing more welcome. He sat down and took my head in his lap and begun to rub my forehead and my eyes, and

I give you my word that with every rub he took a million busting rockets out of the skies.

"Are you in great pain, señor?" says Pepillo, as gentle as a lamb.

"Keep rubbing!" I managed to gasp at him. "And keep talking!"

Now, it may seem queer to you, but the fact is that that smooth, clear voice of the kid was like a staff for me to lean on. Hanging onto that voice was like following a thread that was taking me out of the labyrinth of darkness that I had fallen into.

He wasn't so sassy, now. He seemed to of sobered down a lot, and you would of thought that he was even respectful, to of heard him.

"I thought that you were lost," said Pepillo, still rubbing the busting stars out of the sky, "but it was just as I hoped. When he knocked you down, you stood up stronger than ever! Ah, but when he drove you across the room— every blow that fell on you, it fell on me, also! Por Dios, I still ache with the pain of those terrible strokes! He drove you to the wall—but, ah, the thought of defeat made you a lion again."

"Go on talking," say I, "but don't talk like a fool. I was licked, kid, but when you yelled at me, you let in a flash of light, and I could see to hit him again. Go on talking! Will Rusty fight again?"

"Not if you go back soon enough!" said the kid. "Rusty McArdle is even sicker than you, and he will not be well again, so soon. Because he knows that he was a beaten man. There is a weight on him, be sure, and that weight is the knowledge that you spared him, when you might have struck him down, at the end. It is a weight on the others, also. They could withstand your strength, señor, but they cannot withstand your mercy. It is a club that beats them to the ground. Ah, if I could have told you what to do, I should not have had wit enough to suggest that!"

I was still too groggy to explain in detail. I only mumbled to him that I hadn't finished off Rusty because I was too weak to risk the try. But Pepillo, he only laughed.

"That is the way with genius," said he. "It doesn't understand itself. It lives in a cloud!"

"Lay off from that sort of talk, Pepillo," says I. "Leave

it be, because it don't buy nothing with me. But help me to sit up. I'm better, now!"

He helped to prop me up. I held my head in my hands for a while and then I took hold of his shoulder and managed to get to my feet. I was still wobbly, and I staggered around a bit while he dusted the dirt and the leaves off of me. But pretty soon, I was coming back to myself.

There was two things to buck me up. One was that I wanted to get back inside of the house as soon as I could, before Rusty was shipshape again. The other was that the feeling that I had beat him was like three-fingers of red-eye burning in me and giving me power.

I managed to take a straight step. I dragged down a few clean breaths of air, and then I was ready. Pepillo put the handle of the old Colt in my fingers.

"Go in with this, señor," said he. "They are men of that sort, and they will expect to see a gun, now."

He was right, of course, but the feel of that gun was a nasty thing. However, I had started to work by bluff and I had to keep right on by bluff. So I went up to the front door of the house and I kicked it open and stepped into the living-room, wearing the blackest frown that I could raise.

The boys had been working like mad every minute of the time while I was away. I saw a knot of them around Rusty. They had drenched him with water, and they was fanning him on each side with a couple of coats. Any one of them could of shot my eye-teeth out, and I knew it, but they seemed to think that what I could do with my fists I could do just as well with a gun, and that Rusty was their one good bet against me. So they put their whole risk on him.

But poor Rusty was still at sea. You could tell with one look at him that he was still gone. His jaw was set and his face was pale and sweating, just from the effort that he was making to pull himself together. But it wouldn't work. His eyes was still troubled and empty, and his head wasn't upright on his neck. I figured that I had that trick as good as in my hand.

I walked over and stood above them, glowering blacker than ever.

"We've had it out with the fists, McArdle," says I, "and now we'll have it out with the guns. Stand up!"

"Ay, damn you!" says Rusty. "I'm ready!"

He tried to stand up, but they hauled him down again. Shorty jumped out in front of me. He looked scared. And he was pretty badly marred from his fall down the stairs with two hundred pounds of me on top of him. He held both hands up, as if he wanted to show that he come as peacemaker.

"Chief," says Shorty, "Rusty ain't fit. Bear down light on him, will you? He says he'll fight, but he ain't fit. It would be a murder, and by the cut of your jib I know that you ain't a murderer, Chief."

There was one word in that speech that tickled me, and he had used it twice. When he called me Chief it was as much as to tell me that the boys had done laughing. They had decided to take me serious, and that was almost more than I had been able to pray for, a little while ago.

"If he can't fight," says I, "the rest of you take care of him till he can. Or if there is any of you that the rest would like to elect to step out here and have it out with me with powder and lead, let him talk up. I got a minute or two with nothing on my hands. Step up and take your choice!"

And I started in to walk up and down that big room, paying no attention to them, and my eyes on the watch in my hand. Finally I slammed it into my pocket and whirled around on them. They jumped, and every one of them watched me as though he was seeing a ghost.

"Get out!" says I, and pointed to the door. "Get your McArdle out of this here room and out of this here house. And get quick, because I'm running bank full and I'm about to flood over!"

I knew that there was not one among them that would take talk like that from me, if he was alone, but now they started in to look at each other, and the mob wasn't a quarter as brave as the least brave of the lot of them. They couldn't make up their minds which should start the action, and so each waited for the other fellow; and then the whole lot begun to drift like sheep towards the back door.

It was the prettiest picture that I ever seen in my born days. When they was filing out the back door I hollered: "Shorty!" He was the nerviest of the lot, and so he was the slowest and the last to leave. He started as if a bullet had been jammed through his back. Then he whirled around and faced me, pale but determined looking.

"Come back here!" says I, and I pointed to a spot close up to me on the floor.

His big mouth puckered and his lips curled as he thought of a whole lot of mean things that he might of said. But I suppose that that room looked terrible big and empty to him, and every one of his pals, sneaking away out yonder through the night was taking a part of the courage of Shorty along with him. So he come back and stood right where I had pointed to the place. He didn't stand like any lamb. He stood like a damn wolf, still snarling, but silent.

Yes, Shorty was game, and he was willing to go for his gun right now. I knew it, and I knew that I was standing just three feet and half a second away from my death, if I did the wrong thing, or said it, or made any sort of a false move. Believe me, I didn't intend to take no chances, but still, I wanted to push Shorty just as far as it was safe.

"Shorty," says I, "I come out here having heard a lot of yarns about the gents on this ranch. I'd heard that they was plumb men! I'd heard that they was the toughest, wildest, hardest lot of yeggs that ever got outside of a prison and mobbed together. I've heard that there was no man on the range that could master them!"

That was my beginning, and then I saw Shorty stick out his long jaw and get ready for the shock of hearing how measly and weak and useless I'd really found that crowd that had the famous name for hardness.

But right there, I double-crossed him. I says to Shorty:

"Well, Shorty, I come out here and I found that you all lived right up to your name! Because of all the mean-looking lot of gun-toters I ever seen, you boys are the meanest and most dangerousest!"

You could of flattened Shorty, he was so astonished. He'd just heard from me what he considered about the biggest compliment that any man could pay to that gang of thugs. And then he searched my face to find out what my hidden meanings might be. But I went right on, grinning at him.

"Shorty," says I, "if I was one of the common punchers, working for ordinary pay, I'd reckon to do just about what you boys are doing. But I ain't. I get higher pay, a damned sight, and I get it for running a ranch. Y'understand? I can see how you boys figgered. And I can sympathize with you, a lot. But that ain't my job. I'm here to run this here outfit, and by God, I'm gunna do it! I ain't gunna turn loose the boys that can't get on with me. It would simply mean sending them back into the hills to gang up with the rustlers. No, when I fire one of you gents, it's gunna be fair and square shooting. All I ask is that if one of you drop me, you plant me where I dropped, and stick a shingle in the ground to say that a buckin' hoss got the best of me! And if I manage to drop you boys, I'll do the same by you, honest and faithful, because I live up to my promises."

A grin begun to fight with the wonder in the eyes of Shorty, and I went right on with my speech.

"With a fighting gang like you," says I, "this ranch can be wrecked, or it can be made. If I got you boys behind me, I can make you famous, because we'll go through them mountains like hot shot through butter, and we'll make the rustlers scatter for the lowlands *pronto*. You've been famous for being a mean lot, but I'll make you famous for being something more than mean. Y'understand me, Shorty?"

He looked me fair and square in the face, and oh, but he had a mean eye. He was having a struggle with himself, and asking himself if he could really do anything but hate me with his whole heart! He couldn't make up his mind, right then.

"Go back to the bunkhouse," says I. "Tell the boys what I say. If they'll play the game with me, I'll play the game with them. If they want to down me, let 'em elect their representative, and I'm ready for him, night or day. So long, Shorty!"

He got to the door and then I stopped him again.

"There's one thing that we ain't talked about," says I. "And that's the way you boys have been using this place for a club house. Right now to-night it quits. The niggers are gunna get orders to clean up all of your things that they find in here and take them out to the bunkhouse. And when you're off the range, after this, you're gunna stay in that bunkhouse, and no place else. Because if you come in here, they's gunna be so much trouble, Shorty, that it will make to-night look like a Salvation Army picnic!"

CHAPTER XIV

Shorty didn't answer. He went out with just a black look at me, which was his declaration of independence, as you might say, but I noticed that he didn't slam the door; and at a time like that, actions speak a lot louder than words, of course.

When he was gone, I says to Pepillo: "Kid, pull down the shades!"

But he was already doing it. He skinned around that room, not making no more noise than a blowing feather and here we was with the eyes of the outside world shut away.

"Was it all right?" says I to Pepillo.

He stopped for a minute to consider that, and he shrugged his shoulders with a very Frenchy sort of an expression.

"Oh—it would do!" said Pepillo. "But before you make another speech, let me help you to write it down first! Oh, yes, it was very good, but you could have stepped on them harder. He would have stood for much more than you gave him!"

I had no chance to argue points with Pepillo, because right here, the door opened, and in comes that Randal again. He was smoking a cigar, and he was pretty thoughtful. He walked up and stood looking down at me.

"Well," says Randal, "I'm damned if I know whether you're better as a fighter or as a bluff!"

It made me mad, of course. I only had to look back a very short distance to remember how he had been in a blue funk, but I didn't wish to make trouble just then, because I was feeling weak and comfortable. So I just let myself smile up at Harry Randal. He snarled, and began to pace the room. You would think that I had done him a harm, instead of putting down those wild punchers that he had collected.

Pepillo come and stood just behind my chair with his arms folded on the top of it, which brought his lips pretty close to my ear. He murmured: "This pig is full of wonder. That is why he is nasty. Some pigs are that way, señor!"

"How old are you, Pepillo?" said I.

"I am fourteen, señor," says he.

"You talk like you was forty," says I.

"I have not lived fourteen years in an eggshell," says Pepillo. "Look! The pig is going to ask questions."

Randal turned around and braced his feet. He chawed away at his cigar and frowned at me, like a Yankee salesman.

"Big boy," says he, "when you came into this house, you were scared to death."

"Was I?" says I.

"Don't try to lie out of it," says Randal. "But send that brat away. I want to talk to you."

I was about to do what he wanted, but Pepillo jabbed me with his elbow and whispered behind his hand, "No!"

So I said: "This kid is as tight as a drum. He won't leak any news, if that's what you're afraid of. Besides, I'm used to having him with me."

"Except when you're in jail?" says Randal.

My, what a mean disposition that Randal had!

"You're talking foolish," said I to Randal. "Do you want to make trouble with me?"

He didn't even hear me.

"I can't make it out," he went on. "You came in here shaking, and ten minutes later you come out and slam through the crowd of them, knock three or four down, throw Shorty down the stairs, and beat Rusty McArdle to a pulp. Gad! I didn't think that any man could have done that! What happened to you between the time that you came into the house and the time that you beat McArdle? That's what I can't make out!"

I hadn't thought of it before, but now that I turned my mind backwards, I could see that only one thing had happened, and that was the Blue Jay. It was Pepillo that had made me fight like a crazy man instead of running away as fast as I could, but how could I explain that a kid like him was at the bottom of what I done?

"You wouldn't understand," says I, "if I was to say that I was just thinking things over when I come into the house. As soon as I got something mapped out, I went ahead and did it."

"Bunk!" says Randal. "Purest bunk in the world, and I know it. However—I can't figure it out just yet, but I will sooner or later! There's a secret, somewhere. I can tell by the grin on the face of that brat. However, the next thing to work out is what will you do in the morning?"

"See if the boys will toe the line, and if they will, I start my thinking at that point. I suppose that the rustlers come next. What do you know about them?"

Randal threw up his hands.

"I know too much," says he. "I know, because I heard part of the story from Uncle Stephen, and the rest of it I've worked out myself. I learned about it, because I hoped that I could enable myself to beat the lot of them, once I knew who and what they really were, but the more I've learned, the more hopeless I see that the job is!"

He laid out the whole thing to me, and I repeat it to you, just word for word the way that he said it to me. No, not in the same words, because that would take a lot too long; but I'll tell you all the facts of importance that he gave me. Damned important and damned queer, I thought them!

It seems that back in the beginning, along in the forties or the fifties, whenever it was that the Mexican War came, all of this part of the range belonged to old Mexico, and Sour Creek, and the Sour Creek valley, from the water-divide of one mountain range to the water-divide of the other, all belonged by a Spanish grant to a family by name of Mauricio. Which it's a funny name for a family, ain't it?

Well, after the Mexican War, we Americans come along and thumbed our noses at Mexican ideas in general and Spanish land grants in particular. We grabbed land right and left, and we got rich quick. But up here in the valley of Sour Creek, when the Mauricios were drove out of the valley, they just turned around and went to the mountains, and there they settled down in the cañons and lived off of what the Americans raised in the valleys— like landlords, you understand, except that they collected their rent with a gun. And when people tried to clean out those badlands to the south, they had no luck at all! You could hide a hundred thousand cows in those cañons as easy as if they was grains of sand!

Nobody paid much attention, after a while. From the insides of those mountains, the Mauricios, they lived like lords. They got everything down to a reglar system. From every cattle owner they took a certain amount, and nothing was said, because the cow men all knew that if one rustler was hunted out of those mountains, another rustler was pretty sure to get in. And the great thing about the Mauricios was that they stole in good order. They never took from any one man more'n he could stand; and they never let another rustler poach on their preserves. You might say that they come to have a sort of a legitimate right to rustle on those lands that once belonged to them by right of law.

This lasted until Stephen Randal came along. He didn't give a damn for traditions except the ones that he started himself. The first thing that he done, he shut up the mouths of the cañons that opened into Sour Creek, as well as he could, and he hired about a hundred men for that job. He spent money like water, but he was willing to. Chance give him his innings.

The representative of the Mauricios just then was two brothers, Valentin and Gaspar. Valentin was the smart thinker, and Gaspar was the fighter. Well, this Gaspar by chance got mixed up with Stephen Randal, and Randal shot him dead. That took a lot of the sap out of Valentin Mauricio. He could of gone on poaching in spite of all the men that Randal hired, but he didn't have the hankering to trip up on Steve Randal's big feet.

He drifted south into Mexico, fetching along with him, Leonor, the daughter of that dead Gaspar. Down in Mexico, Valentin tried his hand at legitimate business, but the open range had an attraction for him. He started a silver business—intercepting burro trains carrying high-class ore from the higher mines in the mountains—and he done pretty well, at that trade. But all the time he was hankering to get back to the mountains near Sour Creek—the hereditary domains of the proud old Mauricios, you understand! Only, Valentin Mauricio wanted to have an ally along who would handle Stephen Randal for him.

He found the very man. His niece, Leonor, grew up,

very pretty, so folks said, and that face of hers, it turned the head of the wildest, handsomest, uselessest man in Mexico. I mean, Pablo Almadares!

Maybe you've heard of Pablo Almadares, anyway. He was talked about like something in a story-book, for a while. And he *was* like something out of a book. This Almadares went wild about Leonor. "I'll give you my niece," says this here Valentin Mauricio, "but first you give me a hand up yonder at Sour Creek."

No sooner said than done, as they say in the story. Almadares rode up north with him, and he landed just before Stephen Randal died. Which was too bad, as all hands agreed, because the scrap between them two would of been enough to make you happy to only think about. But of course, Almadares would of won; he always won. However, Randal died in peace, but right after that, Almadares made a great raid and scooped in a tremendous lot of cows, from this and other ranches.

After that, things were quiet. Seemed as though Almadares must of been married and went away to Mexico to enjoy his honeymoon. Only, just lately the trouble started once more, and the cows seemed to be melting away off the range.

CHAPTER XV

That was the frame to the picture that I knew about already, and the frame made a good deal of difference. You can tackle a doctoring case pretty cheerful, when you know that it's just a matter of a broken leg that will knit and get well, or a fever that will burn itself out, but when you come bump up against an incurable, you feel sort of helpless. And here was I engaged in the job of putting a blanket over the head of a firm that had been rustling cows since Noah was a pup, as you might say!

"Now, look here," says I to Randal. "While we're talking about this side of the business, you might as well tell me if there's any watered stock in the business, eh? Because if there is, this is the time to tell me about it before I get my heart all down in my boots, y'understand?"

Which he said that he did, and he wanted to know what I wanted to ask.

"There is American legal tender and there is printed Mexican money," says I. "Sometimes it will take as much as a hundred of them printed dollars to make one American hundred cents. And it's the same way with reputations. A gent that is considered a reglar buster down there south of the Rio Grande, maybe will turn out to be just a cheap skate throwing a bluff when he comes north of the river. Give me the low-down and confess, old timer, that some of these here Mexican badmen are just a lot more Mexican than they are bad; I mean, sneaking and treacherous and low, but not real dangerous to a man—"

"Oh, gringo dog!" moans a voice at my ear. "Then let me tell you that when Pablo Almadares comes to hunt you, you will not stand to fight as you did against Señor

McArdle, but you will turn and run like a whipped coyote. But then you will see how quickly and how easily he will catch you, and how he will kill you, because you are gringo! gringo! gringo! And a pig!"

That was the report from Pepillo. I forgot about him being a Mexican. It made me feel pretty cheap and bad, too.

"Pepillo," says I, "you damn little Blue Jay, I forgot that you might belong to any one race. I looked on you like you was a bird of all the feathers that they is. I forgot that you was a greaser. But you're an exception. The rest of them are nothing, but you're the bright and shining exception, Pepillo, in a line of bad sports!"

I thought that that, maybe, would soothe him down, a good deal, but I had riled him so bad, now, that his steam was near the busting point.

"We do not live for filthy dollars, I thank God!" says Pepillo. "We live for glory, and Mexico—Mexico—is a nation of warriors!"

Why, to see that imp stand there and throw back his head and almost close his eyes with happiness, you would think that there was really nothing but pity to be had for everything and everybody that wasn't Mexican.

Then he opens his eyes wide and glares at me.

"But you—Yankee pig—Yankee dog—faugh!—I hate you—like the dirt under my feet!"

He whirled around and made for the door.

"Look here, Pepillo," says I, "damn it, I'm sorry!"

He didn't look, though. He was through the door in a flash and then he was up the stairs. I went after him like a steam engine. Slam went the door of my room in my face and the lock clicked.

"Pepillo" says I, "are you gunna be a damn little fool and run away?"

"What matter does it make?" says Pepillo. "I am only a greaser! I am only a Mexican! What difference does it make to you what I do?"

"Kid," says I, "if you start crying, I'm gunna bust down the door."

I had made another wrong step. He simply yelled with anger.

"I am *not* crying!" shouts Pepillo. "Except for anger that such a lump of a creature should have shamed me! I should have driven my knife into your back! I am *not* crying!"

All this, with his voice wobbling back and forth, very hard to keep from a squawk one minute and a moan the next.

"Pepillo," says I, shaking the lock of that door, "I apologize. I want you to forgive me. I am sorry!"

"Do I care if you are sorry?" says Pepillo. "No, I do not care. I shall never see your face again!"

I thought it over. There wasn't any doubt that I was fond of the little devil and that he had worked his way right into my heart. Besides that, I had got to leaning tremendous on him. You simply wouldn't believe how I had got into the habit of turning to him when I wanted to have any thinking done for me. But I could see that Pepillo was spoiled pretty bad. I had made so much of him that if I kept on soothing him and petting him, he would pretty soon be too hot for me to handle, altogether.

So I says: "You suit yourself. I'm sorry that I run down your country. I'd hate to have you leave me. I'm mighty fond of you, kid. But I ain't gunna treat you like a baby. You can beat it when you get ready, but once you go, you can damn well make sure that I won't never come begging you to come back to me!"

I heard a ring of mocking laughter from the inside of the room that went through me like an echo in an empty house, and when I got down the stairs, I was pretty blue.

Randal was staring and sneering when I got down to the living-room.

"You been up there babying that kid?" says he. "If any brat said half that much to me, I'd bust him in two and nail the halves on two posts. You make a fool of yourself, big boy."

I couldn't trust myself to speak. Somehow, it made me so mad to have that Harry Randal tell me how I had ought to treat Pepillo, that I couldn't risk speaking, because one word would have let me explode, and then I would of gone for Randal, you know. So I only gave him a mean look—but there was enough meanness in that look to calm him down again.

He said: "Let's get back to the thing that we were talking about. You were asking about the Mexicans in this deal—were they real men or just fakers?"

"That's it, and it makes a lot of difference."

"Well," said Randal, "I don't know what part of the range you were brought up on, but for my part, I know that an average Mexican is about as strong, as brave, as tough, and as mean as any Yankee that ever lived. I know it because I've been around them all of my life. But maybe you've had a different experience with them."

I had. Mexicans was always partial to me as a pin-cushion, except that the pins that they tried to stick in me was always made of steel ground to a sharp point, and mostly long enough to kill. Right down to the kid, there was always knives in the air when I come across a greaser.

And I hate knives. I hate them worse than I hate poison. Because you can stand up and fight fair with fists or clubs or guns, but somehow to run a knife like a long tooth into the flesh of another human being—why, it always makes me feel sick and dizzy, and that's a fact.

I just said: "They like knives, and I'd kill a man that pulled a knife on me!"

"Did you ever kill a man for a thing like that?" says Harry Randal, not loud enough to disturb me much.

"I killed five for it," says I, "and maybe I'll kill some more before I—"

"I stopped myself after I realized that I had already said too much. I got up and glared at Randal, but he was very pleased with himself, and he leaned back and rubbed his hands together, most contented.

"All right," says Randal. "I've got a close mouth. *I* won't talk about you. But it seems that there was parts of your history that the judge didn't know anything about, eh? What you did in the city was really just a little vacation party. While you were away from work? Don't mention it, big boy. Only, I see that you have reason for hating the greasers. I suppose that some of them don't love you, either!"

I had to admit: "They hate me all the way to Mexico City. I'm proud of it, but I got to admit that I lose a little sleep over it. But what about this Valentin Mauricio and Pablo Almadares?"

"Valentin," said Harry Randal, "is a cool fellow with a sharp head on his shoulders. He knows how to take care of himself, but he isn't aggressive unless he has somebody else to do the fighting for him. His brother, Gaspar, was a regular bulldog, and he executed the plans that Valentin made for him.

"Pablo Almadares is a different matter. He is a gentleman who turned crook for the pleasure that it brought to him. They say that he has a very honorable name and a still more honorable estate somewhere down in old Mexico, as well as a lot of the pure Castilian in his veins—you know what I mean. But this Almadares was born to love trouble for its own sake. He likes a fight. He likes it better than you and this Rusty McArdle rolled into one. And he finds his fights, too. They have a price on his head and in half a dozen states the governors will pay out a fat bonus on top of the Federal reward. There's nothing particularly vicious about this Pablo Almadares. But dangerous? Oh, man, it was when I heard about Pablo Almadares that I started in to give the boys their own way on my ranch. Better for them to take liberties than for Almadares to take the whole damned place and the cows that are on it!"

Now, it has always seemed to me that you can make a difference between reality and imitation. Out of two imitations, one may look bad and the other seem more real, but when the important reality itself comes along, you don't have to use your reason none. A gong rings inside of you, and you know that this is the hundred per cent fact that you got your hands on.

It was that way when I listened to that Randal. He was a faker, but when he talked about Almadares, he sure had the golden ring in his voice. Yes, sir, I knew that if I had to mingle with that Pablo, it would be an awful mess all around!

CHAPTER XVI

You will notice that in all of this Randal had controlled his joy pretty well on the subject of how I had handled Rusty McArdle and the rest. But I didn't hold that against him. You can't expect a pint measure to hold a bushel, and there simply wasn't room in Randal for anything generous, like praise. What he aimed at was to show me that I had simply managed to finish off the first bit of my job, with a lot worse stuff coming along behind it.

I forgot about him the minute that I left the room. I had stayed away a lot longer than I intended, and right then I would rather of lost my hopes of that ranch than to of give up that kid—he meant so much to me.

I tried my door and found it locked, just the same as it had been before—and there was no lamplight leaking out through the crack beneath the door. That looked bad. I went out around the house and when I come opposite my window, my toe chinked on a bit of metal. I scooped it up, and it was the key to my room!

That made me feel worse than ever, because it was easy to figure that the kid had climbed down the drainage pipe—which would be plumb easy for an active little monkey like him—and then he had dropped my key and started away.

I climbed up the pipe, simply because it was a good deal quicker than going clear around to go up the stairs and open the door from the outside. When I shoved my head through the window I got a happy surprise. There wasn't much of a moon out—just a thin half circle a quarter of the distance up the sky—but it gave enough light to show me Pepillo lying on his face on the bed.

He jumped up right away when he seen me and he hollers out:

"I desire to leave this room, señor! I—I have lost the key—and—and I dared not venture down the outside from the window. Otherwise you should never have seen me again, gringo devil!"

The darkness covered up my grin, and I was glad of that. Because if he had suspected that I saw through him, it would certainly have been the end between me and the kid. However, it *was* easy to tell what had happened. He had lost his nerve about leaving the house and me, and so he had thought of this dodge to keep himself there: throwing the key out of the window, first, so that it would be lost, and then pretending that he was afraid to climb down to the ground!

All of this flashed on me, but what I see most clearly was that the best way for me to get rid of the kid forever would be to let him see, now, how I could look through him. And you can believe that I didn't want to get rid of him!

So I just says: "All right, old son, but where did you think that you might of left the key?"

"If I could tell that, señor," says Pepillo, "should I not have found it at once and let myself escape from this house and from you and from all the other gringos, whom I hate forever?"

"That's pretty mean talk, Pepillo," says I. "But I wish that you would forget what I said a while back. I tell you, Pepillo," says I, sitting down on a chair as close to him as I dared, "that everybody has a different way of looking at folks. You take a high-class, educated gent that has traveled a lot, and he is always pretty easy on foreigners. It doesn't make any difference to him if a man talks in a queer way or wears funny clothes or eats with the handle of his fork. Y'understand? But you take a low-down common sort of a gent that ain't traveled much, he don't take to strange things—not at all, he don't! What he wants is his own kind of pork and beans, or else he pretty near starves to death. And you take him when he meets up with a fellow that wears clothes different to him, and talks a different language, and walks in a different way, why he just about hates that gent—and if he don't laugh at him, he wants to about kill him. Well, Pepillo, I'm just one of them low-down, ignorant folks that ain't had no education, you see. I suppose that I ain't got much against the greasers—I mean, the Mexicans—but they got a tricky way with their knives, you got to admit, and after a fellow has been carved up a few times, you understand—"

"Ah, ah," says Pepillo, "have you been stabbed by one of my countrymen?"

"Have I been stabbed by one of your countrymen?" says I. "I'll tell a man that I been stabbed by one of your countrymen! Lemme show you!"

I lighted the lamp and when it was going good, I turned around to Pepillo. He kept back in the shadow, which I could see that he didn't want to come too close to me, and that made me wonder a good deal. But I showed him a place on the inside of my left hand, first, where there was a big white scar, caused by taking hold of the knife of a greaser that was kneeling on my chest, just then!

"Well," says Pepillo, very edgy, "do you go about taking knives of fighting men in your hand?"

"This gent," says I, "was sitting on my chest, just then, and one of his pals was a-hold of my two feet and a cousin of his was trying to find a gun that had dropped on the floor, so's he could come over and make sure of killing me!"

"Por Dios!" gasped Pepillo.

And he comes out into the light to stare at me and the cut on my hand. Then, when the lamplight hit him fair, I could see why was it that Pepillo had wanted to keep in the shadow. Because his eyes, they was all rimmed with red, and I could see that he must of been lying up there bawling most of the time that I was away, until maybe he cried himself to sleep. It softened me down a good deal to see that, just as it would of softened you down, maybe. He was a good kid, you understand, and I could tell that he was fond of me just as I was of him, only not so much, of course. Him and me had been through a lot together, this same day!

"But how did you escape?" cried Pepillo. "But you had other friends in that place and they came to you with help?"

"The four of us was alone," says I, "excepting for a fifth man that didn't count, because I'd hit him in the right place when his pals was putting me down."

"But with three men—and you on the floor—and the knife flashing above you—Señor Kitchin!" sings out the kid.

And doggone me if he didn't put his hands together and begin to wring them like the knife was in danger of driving through *him!* He was a funny one, was that Blue Jay, and not like neither man or boy.

"I grabbed at the knife as it come down," I told him, "and turned it away from my throat, which he was aiming at. Then I kicked the other Mexican off my feet and into the wall. That gave me a chance to tear into the boy that was on my chest. I rolled him into the wall, too, and slammed Mexican number three in the face, and after that, I was able to dive through the window and get away. I tied a half of my shirt around my hand, but I was bled weak before I could get to the doctor, five miles away—and there you are for *one* reason why I don't love Mexicans, Pepillo!"

His eyes was closed and he was shuddering.

"Ah, ah!" says the Blue Jay. "I begin to understand!"

"And here's another to show you," says I, and I opens up my shirt and shows him a place across my chest and the right side of my ribs where a bowie knife had gone slithering. Pepillo's eyes was as big as saucers.

"That was your life!" cried he. "And how many lives have you, Amigo!"

"That was one of the nine," I admitted. "I'll tell you about that. I had got it in for the gentleman greasers by that time, but the ladies still looked pretty good to me, and there was a little beauty by name of Maria something-or-other, living over in San Sebastian. I used to wade my hoss across the river and go to see her." I could see a pretty cold look in the face of the kid, and I wondered at it. I went on: "If there was only a light in the living-room window, then I knew that I could go on up to the house. But if there was a light in the kitchen, too, then I could know that her suitor was there. Because her family had it fixed how they was to splice her to a rich young don from down the country. Mateo was his name, I think. I forget what else. But I got tired of seeing the lights in both of the windows, and so I laid for this here Mateo, one night, and pulled him off his hoss and took him down to the edge of the river.

" 'Mateo,' says I, 'you're a pretty fine-looking chap and I would sure hate to have you found drowned by accident in the river. But I would like to know how did you ever get that bad habit of coming to visit Maria? She's plumb unhealthy for you!"

"This Mateo, he wasn't any fool. He says: 'I tell you by the truth of God, señor, that I have already been feeling the damps of this air in the lowlands. The house is too close to the river. And the marshes are full of a deadly malaria, and other fevers, are they not?'

"I admitted that the climate was pretty near sure to be fatal to him, and he agreed with me and thanked me for showing him the facts. So I let him up and put him back on his horse. And he rode off—"

"Ah, the coward!" pipes Pepillo.

"He stops at a little distance and turns loose some lead at me," says I, "but nothing hit me. Because, you know, your countrymen, they ain't as handy with guns as they are with knives. But my Maria, when the don stopped paying attentions to her, she located the trouble and found out that I had scared him away. She took very kind to that idea, although it made her pa and ma pretty cross. But one evening while we was sitting under the big cypresses down by the edge of the river, holding hands and the rest of it—"

"And the rest of what!" busts in Pepillo, very sharp.

"Why, making love, of course, you young sap!" says I. "Did you think that I was taking those long rides for the sake of a glass of wine and some talk about the weather? Because if you did, think again. It's your turn!"

"I see," says Pepillo. "You were what you call spooning, no?"

"All right," says I. "You may call it that, if you want to. I had just been telling Maria that I loved her more than any other woman was even able to imagine being loved—"

"Was not that false?" busts in Pepillo.

"Oh, sure," says I, "but you know how it is—or you will know when you get about two or three years older. You got to talk sort of foolish to a girl or she don't understand."

"Faugh!" says Pepillo. "It fills me with a great disgust! Are all men like you?"

"Sure," says I, "only worse. That is, most of them are, and them that ain't, would be if they could. I ain't done much harm to the ladies, because God didn't give me the face for it. However, I was telling you that I was finished with telling Maria how she come like an angel into my life—and all that sort of bunk, y'understand—and Maria, she comes back with: 'Alas, my dear, but I fear that my father and mother will never let me marry you!"

"It staggered me, sort of, and I popped out: 'Marriage!'

" 'Dios!' says Maria. 'Do you not intend to marry me?'

" 'Dios!' says I. 'But of course I do!'

" 'Then,' says Maria, 'there is only one way. You must come and carry me away, my love, some night. You must come with two fleet horses. And I shall bring down enough of my father's money to make a dowry—'

"It flabbergasted me! 'Sure,' says I. 'To-morrow night I'll be here; at midnight, Maria.'

"But of course, when to-morrow night come, I was not at her father's house."

"It was because you would not have her to steal her father's money, was it not?" says Pepillo, very eager.

"Hell, kid," says I, "why would I be saddled with a greaser for a wife?"

Pepillo jumped up and stamped.

"Gringo dog!" yells he. "They are far, far above you!"

"Sure," says I, very quick. "Sure they are above me. But that's the reason that I wouldn't marry one of them. I want somebody that is down on my own level, Blue Jay."

"Ah, well," says the Blue Jay, "you are nothing but great lies, one on top of the other. But what has all of this to do with the knife-wound?"

"I'm coming to it," says I. "You see, that next night, I thought that I would try to fill the gap that was left in my heart by the losing of Maria—"

"Bah! You have no heart!" snaps Pepillo.

"All right," says I. "Anyway, I was looking for amusement, and then I remembered me of a blue-eyed little Irish girl living up in the hills. A great card she was, and a hand at jigging such as you never seen or guessed about, old timer! So I went up to see the Irish kid, and when I come back, it was pretty late. And when I come to my quarters it was close to dawn, and against the grey of the morning light, I seen a shadow that come jumping at me. I fetched up an arm to guard myself, but I was too late. A knife blade sank into my breast and the hilt thumping home. And if it hadn't been that the point of the knife turned along my ribs instead of slipping between them, I would of been a tolerable dead Blondy Kitchin, before the sun come up!"

"It was Maria!" says the kid.

"It was her, all right."

"She was right!" says Pepillo. "If a man jilts a woman, it is her *duty* to kill him!"

"You're like all kids," says I to him. "All wild about your ideas of women. All wild and wrong, old son. Anyway, that was Maria, right enough. I barely had time to get her out of the room, because she'd turned hysterical and was swearing that she would kill herself because she had killed me. But I took the knife away from her and told her that it wasn't more than a scratch, and that she had only made herself mighty ridiculous. That turned her mad again, because there ain't nothing that a woman likes more than to be grand and heroic and passionate and mean, y'understand—"

"Stuff!" says Pepillo. "It is plain that you have never known ladies, señor!"

"No, maybe they're different," says I, "but it always looks to me that they been all painted with the same kind of tar! Anyway, that Maria put me in bed for three weeks, and damned if there wasn't a funny thing, Pepillo. She sent me flowers every doggone day, and used to come and sit by the window, looking very pretty!"

"Did that seem strange to you?" says Pepillo, very sneering.

"Sure it did—pretty near crazy," says I.

"And yet you say that you understand women!" says Pepillo. "Bah!"

"Anyway," says I, "when I got well, I had to skin out of that part of the country, because I begun to suspect that if I didn't look out, that Maria would marry me, whether I wanted to or not! However, that cured me of Mexican girls, same as I had been cured of the Mexican men, before. However, I want to show you where a bunch of Mexican gamblers went after me, down in a dive on the river. I beat them off with a chair till I got a little clearance, but when I tried to jump through the window, one of them dived in quicker than a snake strikes and he sank his knife right into my hip. Lemme show you that scar, because it's a beauty. Twists clear around to the back of my leg!"

But Pepillo, he held up both his hands and closed his eyes and shook his head.

"No more, señor!" says he. "All of this talk, it sickens me a little. I do not like blood. No, but I dread and I hate it! I do not wish to see any more of your wounds. But alas,

Señor Kitchin, how many times you have been at the very edge of dying, have you not!"

"I got to admit it," says I. "I been mighty close enough times."

Pepillo got very earnest.

"It is this that you must know," says he. "There are two bloods in Mexico. There is the true Spanish blood, and there is the Indian blood. Alas, the blood of the Spaniard is not as much as we might wish. And there is mostly the blood of the Indians, they are what you find Indians everywhere—brave, wild, strange, savage like tigers! But the Spanish blood—"

"Tell me, Pepillo," says I, "is there any Indian in you?"

"Not one drop!" says the kid, and I believed him, because his skin, though it was olive colored, was wonderful clear. "But as for the harms that my people have done you, Señor Kitchin, I am sorry!"

"Kid," says I, "they never done me so much harm as you've done me good. Shake on it!"

Which we done, and it was great to be friends again.

CHAPTER XVII

When Pepillo set his mind on it, he could manage more things than you would ever guess. My face was bunged up pretty bad, and it was either purple and blue or else it was swelling and red, where those fists of Rusty McArdle had banged home. There was still a wavering feeling in the back of my head, and I could tell well enough that if he had happened to land one clean wallop, while he was well set, he would have knocked me out proper and right on the spot. Pepillo made me lie down, and then he begun to work on my face with cold dressings, until the pain and the swelling went down simply wonderful. And after that, he got out a little bottle of a strong liniment which it would make you jump to have it rubbed on your skin, it was so hot! When he was done, I was so relieved and so tired that I pretty near wasn't able to get out of my clothes and into bed.

But Pepillo, he wouldn't sleep on the bed, though there was oceans of room in it. He said that he had slept out so long that beds was a terrible bore to him. And so he just took a big sheepskin rug that was on the floor and rolled himself up in it, and he slept there. That was like him, as you might say. Always doing something different from everybody else!

I barely turned over and got my eyes closed when there came a rap on the door and the voice of one of the niggers saying: "Breakfast in twenty minutes, suh."

"You damn black thief!" says I. "You call this a joke to wake a man up in the middle of the night—and—"

"Señor!" says Pepillo. "Open your eyes!"

I opened 'em, and doggone me if it wasn't broad daylight, and the sky in the east all covered with rose and a cloud hanging there over the rising sun so bright you wouldn't believe it. Pepillo, he looked like he had been up for an hour. He was as fresh as a daisy, and you wouldn't think that him and me had been through a couple of furlongs of hell only the day and the night before! He says that he was going out to look the place over and so I got up and washed and shaved.

That liniment of the kid's was powerful hot, but it was powerful good. It had taken all the swellings and most of the soreness out of the flesh of my face. Only for a spot on the temple and a couple more along the chin where there was still black and blue marks, I was pretty much as though I hadn't stood up the night before to the hardest punching two-fisted man that I ever met in my life. Matter of fact, you would have to look close at my face to see even *them* traces.

I had finished shaving and was about to get into my coat, when I hear a voice roar out and then a terrible cursing, and a sort of a squeal that come out of Pepillo, I gathered.

My first step got me to the head of the stairs. My second one landed at the bottom of them. My third step brought me plumb outside of the house and there I seen that dozen of hard-boiled cowpunchers standing around and laughing their heads off while Shorty swarmed up a tree, swinging himself along wonderful fast with those long, gorilla arms of his, and just half a reach ahead of him went the kid, climbing fast, too, but losing in the race, and yelling his head off for help.

"Señor! Señor Kitchin! He will murder me!"

He sees me and wastes time to throw out an imploring hand towards me, and Shorty gives me an ugly sideglance, too. And I seen those cowpunchers standing around, looking at me like so many foxes. They wondered what I was gunna do about the kid, which they knowed that he was a pet of mine.

But there ain't nothing like favoritism to spoil a crew in a ranch. Besides, I seen that the kid had something coming to him.

I yells out: "I'm home base, Pepillo. You get to me, and you're safe. Shorty won't bother you none, but as long as you're roamin' around, free, he's got his sporting chance at you, and if he tags you, I reckon that you sure will be it!"

It tickled the cowpunchers. They yelled like a lot of wolves. They liked that decision of mine. But then they knew, just as I knew, that no snip of a kid can be allowed to walk up and welt a man in the face, the way that the kid had done to Shorty last night, and get away with it the next day.

Pepillo, he squealed louder than the rest: "I am betrayed! Ah, señor, have mercy! Have mercy! He will kill me!"

I was kind of afraid that he would, too. Shorty wasn't never no beauty winner, but when he climbed up that tree he sure did look like a free-hand sketch of the devil going after a damned soul. If he laid those big hands of his on the kid, bones was sure to snap. However, Pepillo had to have his lesson some day.

The way that Pepillo swarmed up that tree was a caution, but still I wondered how he managed to keep out of the grip of Shorty. Pretty soon, he threw himself out to the end of a big branch and there he hung by his hands from pretty near the tip of it. Shorty went right out after him.

"Shorty!" yells the kid. "If the branch breaks, we'll both be killed!"

"What's that to me?" says Shorty. "So long as I send you to hell before me!"

He meant it, too. He'd been brooding on two things, I suppose. One was the way he'd been thrown downstairs and the other was the way the kid had hit him, and since he couldn't very well take it out of me, he poured all of his broodings onto the head of Pepillo.

"Señor Kitchin!" yells Pepillo to me.

I was scared, and I was sick. It looked like a death, to me.

"Shorty!" yells big McArdle, coming into view for the first time. "Leave the kid be. Get back, or you'll have him dead—"

"I'll run my own business!" says Shorty.

"Get back, damn you!" roars Rusty McArdle, and damned if he didn't pull a gun.

"You dog, you shoot!" yells Shorty, and he worked himself further out on the branch. I think that McArdle *would* of shot, too—for a leg, maybe—because it sure looked as though the kid would fall and break his neck.

But I grabbed the revolver, and I said: "Rusty, it's fine of you to want the kid to have a square chance. I like him better than you do, but he's a boy and he's got to fight himself out of the dirty holes that he gets into."

"All right, Chief," says Rusty, and he puts away his gun. "I guess that it ain't gunna be so hard for you and me to understand each other, after all!"

The kid, up there swinging in the air, seen his last hope go when McArdle put away his Colt. Then the big hand of Shorty reached for him.

I didn't think that *any* kid had that much nerve in him, but Pepillo did. He would rather die than let Shorty grab him. He loosed his hold on the end of the branch and he dropped straight for what looked sure death to me.

But it wasn't! He grabbed at a branch that was a little beneath him. It was only a flying grip he got, and it was broke, at once, but that grip broke the fall for him, and he fell the rest of the way and landed like a cat.

Shorty was behind him, dropping through the tree like a monkey from branch to branch, but when Shorty hit the ground, the kid was already half way towards me, and though Shorty followed him like a fish jumping clear of water, Pepillo came like a bird on wings, half scared and half tickled with the excitement.

When he got to me, he grabbed hold on my belt and stood dancing with fear and pleasure and thumbing his nose at Shorty.

Shorty, with the blood in his face, and his eyes bulging with it, too, pawed for a minute at his belt, and I had an idea that I might have to go for my gun, too. Which would have been the end of me on that ranch, and most like, the end of me anywhere. Because when it come to shooting, I couldn't keep with fast company like all of them boys was.

Who would you think would help me out of a mean hole like that one? Why, you could guess in a million years, so I got to tell you that it was big Rusty McArdle. He speaks up and says:

"Don't throw yourself away, old kid. Just use the bean. The big boy, he give you your chance at Pepillo, didn't he? Now you play white man and give the kid his chance, too!"

It took Shorty a while to work himself out of his fighting trance. He was like that. He liked a fight so well that when he got worked up to the pitch, it was hard for him to ease down. He simply swelled up with a fighting meanness and then he would shiver and shake all over, and sway from side to side and roll his eyes until he was a nightmare to look at, you can bet.

He was like that as he faced Pepillo and me. Then he throwed his eye over towards the rest of the boys, as if he wanted to take their vote, and they all said the same thing:

"You've had your chance, Shorty. Play white, now, and let the kid have a show, will you?"

Shorty mopped his forehead. Then he walked up to me a long, waddling step.

"Big Boy," says he—that Randal seemed to have got the name ready for circulating among them—"Big Boy, I give the gents the word that you passed on to me. And last night we decided that we'd see you damned before we'd see ourselves licked out of the house and still go on working—least of all for you! Well, I dunno how the rest of them figure, just now. But I got this to say: You give me justice with the kid, there, and it sure pleases me a lot. Big Boy, I'm gunna stay on with you and work for you, and I don't give a damn what the rest of them want! The bunkhouse is plenty good enough for me!"

I could have blessed Shorty for that little speech of his. It might be that some of the others would be proud about buckling under to me, but after Shorty had set them the example, I thought that it would be a whole lot easier for them.

Shorty went on: "All I got to say is, that that kid has got something coming to him, and when I catch him alone, I'm going to give it to him. Does that go with you?"

"Shorty," says I, "you seen me act about it once, already. And I ain't changed. Sure, I know that the kid has got something coming to him. You're dead right. While he's around me, me being his pal, you'll let him be. But if you catch him alone, you're free to give him hell! That's a fair and square deal!"

Pepillo, he wrinkled up his face and begun to chatter but Rusty McArdle says: "Shut up, Pepillo. You ought to have about half your acreage of hide quirted off of your back. Big Boy, after what happened last night, I figured that the only way that I could ever look you in the face would be down the barrel of a gun. Well, old son, I dunno that I feel the same way about it, now. Last night you give me a licking that I'm free to say was the first that I ever got! I dunno. I thought at the time that there was a little luck in it. If I'd saved myself and gone easier, I might of knocked you cold. But that's done. I *didn't*. Now, Big Boy, I dunno that I'm good for much on a range. I can't sling a rope and I ain't any hand at riding range, but if you got any uses that I'm fit for, I'll stick around the same as the rest."

It scared me, I tell you, to hear him talk like that. What would I of done in the same place? Why, I would of packed my blanket roll and started south in the night, or if I had the nerve to stay at all, it would have been to fight all over again. But there was something different in Rusty McArdle. He'd been through the grind in the ring, and he seemed to know what it was to fight, and take a thumping and come back like a man. I respected him a lot. I shook hands with him, and I said:

"Rusty, I never seen a man that I was gladder to have under me. Never in my life. The kind of cows that I want you to ride herd on don't wear horns, and they don't eat grass. You know what I mean. I need you a lot. Outside of me, there is only one gent that you got to take orders from on this ranch; meaning an old pal of yours—Shorty. Because he's the assistant."

You might say that I had made a quick and a queer choice for foreman, but I hadn't. I had worked it all over in my head. Maybe Shorty didn't know as much about cows as he might. But that didn't worry me none. I knew enough about them to serve the needs of that ranch. Except when I was off prospecting, I had worked cows all my life. When I seen a cow a mile off shaking her head, I could tell by the way that she shook it, what was wrong with her. I could take one feel of the wind and know when it was strong enough to start steers drifting. And I knew a lot of other things that you got to be partly born to and partly raised to or else you won't never learn them from books or from what other folks have to say. My ideal foreman in that lot was Rusty, but it would of been a joke to appoint him, he was so green on the range. And no matter how the facts turned out, I wanted those boys to think that their main job was to ride range, and their second job—a lot less important than the first—was to see that they kept down the varmints that destroyed the calf crop—wolves or men! Now, next to Rusty McArdle, it was plain that the natural leader in that pack of thugs was Shorty, and so he was my man. Shorty was the most surprised of the lot when he heard me speak. But it was plain that I had pleased the boys, and it was plain that I had pleased Rusty. I have no doubt that he thought that he would have a pretty slick and easy job, now that his old pal was in the saddle. I didn't care about that. What I wanted was harmony, and fighting men!

"Big Boy," says McArdle, "this all sounds to me. I'm with you."

And since my hands was still in his, he closed down on me with all his might!

That was foolish of Rusty—damned foolish. His strength was in his weight *and* his speed. You know how it is—ten pounds is as heavy as twenty, if it's moving twice as fast. That was Rusty's power—his ability to get his weight under way fast and keep it going at a sprinter's gait. But when it come to main might of hand for heaving or hauling or lifting, that natural strength of his wasn't in it with muscles that had been made by swinging double-jacks or bulldogging yearlings. Not in it for a minute!

I took the full power of his grip without half trying, and then I closed back on him—

Not all the way. I could of made him drop down on his knees and yell with pain, but the minute that I felt his knuckles grinding together, I turned loose his hand quick.

"All right, Rusty," says I.

"All right, Big Boy," says he.

And the beauty of it was that nobody else that was there, suspected anything. Because it all happened in five seconds.

However, I'd seen the pain and the surrender in the eyes of McArdle, and I knew that since I'd beaten him a second time, there would not be much spirit in him for trying me a third time, with weapons that would fit him on his feet, without disgracing him before the boys. I figured that he would be grateful for that. I figured that he was too clean and decent, inside of him, not to *want* to pay me back like an honest man!

CHAPTER XVIII

For three days, I was in the saddle or driving in a buckboard about twenty hours per diem. But I hardly knew when to quit, because I never felt tired.

Suppose that somebody asked you to step into a room that was filled with gold that *might* be yours some day. Could you get tired counting it? That was the way that I felt when I rode over that range. I tell you honest that there was never nothing made in the way of a range that could of had it beat. There was never nothing! It had trees enough. It had good fences, and it had plenty of them. It had oceans of water, in the right places. It had a good bunkhouse, a fine ranch-house, of course, and what was more to the business point of view, it had lots of fine roomy, warm-built sheds where if an extra bad winter came, you could close up every last head of stock on your place.

It was stocked with A No. 1 cows; Herefords, mostly. There's some like that Durhams better, but gimme the Herefords. I know them, and they know me, as you might say, and I've got me a good market with Herefords, when I've seen Durhams go begging. That's my experience, and speaking personal, I don't give a damn for the books that might disagree with Experience. That ranch was stocked with fine cows, had a good crop of calves coming on, a fair to middling lot of yearlings, and a whopping bunch of two-year-olds; and besides that, there was some bulls that would of been blue-ribbon winners in any cattle show this side of Mars.

In addition to that, every day that I rode that range, I got to see the value of the hands that were working the place for me. I've showed you their seamy side: but out on the range, riding hell-bent, it was a different story, by a long way. There wasn't no chapter heading in it that was the same. Their meanness turned into courage, then their foxiness turned into good cowcraft; and their strength kept them riding as long and as hard as though they expected to own that ranch, one day, instead of me.

They thrived on work. That was one trouble with Randal. He'd been so afraid of them that to get their favor he had given them light work, and of course that was the sure way to get the opposite thing. It gave them leisure and it gave them energy in their leisure to think up trouble for themselves and everybody else. You can bet that when they got to the end of the day's riding for me, they was barely strong enough to pull the saddle off of their hosses, and sit through their suppers—and, at the end of the day, I kept out of their way. They was mean enough to take any man's head off, beginning with mine. Every evening, I was the meanest and the worst slave-driver of a boss that ever worked the range; but in the morning they'd slept off their grouch, they realized that they was pushing ahead the work on the ranch at a great rate, and they was glad to hop into their saddles again. I tell you, they was such men that they got proud of the rate that they wore out their saddle-strings. Even Rusty, which you would of thought that he was a lot too smart to be so childish, would begin to boast about the way which he had used up hosses riding that range.

In those three days we caught up about half the ends of work that had been allowed to fall loose during the time that Randal was running the ranch, and believe me, that was a lot! I had to begin to give the hosses extra feeds of grain, and Randal kicked a lot at that.

"Catching up in the ranch work isn't what counts," he told me. "That's piddling, small business. The main thing is that old man Henry Randal will be over here in a few days, and when he comes he'll have a count of the cows, and when he makes that count, he's gunna find that we're about a hundred short. The one main thing for you to do is to get those cows replaced. Y'understand? And the next big thing is for you to block up the mouths of those cañons that yawn onto the range from the mountains."

You might say that he was right. And I knew it. But in the meantime, the tools that I had to use for the bigger work needed sharpening. And I was aiming to temper those tools all over again, sharpen them to a good, biting edge, and then see what I could do with them. There's no use trying to break ground with dull drills, as any fool knows! And I was getting my results. For three days the boys was tired, sore, and mean. Then they begun to buck up. They got lean and hard and active, again. They didn't talk so much, which is a good sign. And when they had any spare time, you would see them getting out with their guns and blazing away at anything for a target. Not publicly, but on the side, as you might say. Which showed that I hadn't pulled the wool over their eyes. They knew that when the pinch came the big job would probably have to be done with Colts and Winchesters.

But, in the meantime, they were seeing that I knew my business. They were getting to know every nook and corner of the range. They were getting to know the cows, and they were taking a mighty big interest in their work. When you hear a puncher come in for noon and tell the boys at the table all about how he worked a bogged yearling out of the mud, and when the rest of the boys are willing to set there and listen, then you know that you have your men in the right humor for their work—and that was the way that it was with that crew.

At the end of the week, I had things about where I wanted them, and I took the boys on their first spin into the limestone cañons that looked out of the face of the southern mountains. And that day we found out why it was that the ranch had been left alone for so long and the rustlers hadn't bothered us none. It was a queer story and the way that we come at it was queer, too! I'll tell you about it.

That evening, I took the boys down to the head of the range and we camped near the beginning of Sour Creek. The next morning we lit out on our best ponies. Shorty and a dumpy, dark-faced gent by name of Hawkes was riding in the lead, and when they turned a corner of the ravine that we was in, I heard one of them sing out, and then a gun barked.

We got around that corner in a bunch, with spurs and quirts going, and there we seen, in the near distance, three gents pelting away for the tall timber. Just before they got out of sight around the next bend, Shorty tries a snap shot and the bullet made the horse of one of the three rear and plunge, and the gent that was in the saddle flopped on the rocks.

His hoss couldn't of been bad hurt, because it ran right on out of sight, but the rider lay where he fell. When we got to the spot, the three hosses and the other two riders was gone out of view, complete; and a shower of lead come from some high rocks, to show where they had gone for shelter.

I'll tell you how fit my boys was. They wanted to rush those rocks right off, but I wouldn't let them. I showed them that if the pair of yeggs wanted to, they could pick off the lot of us while we was climbing to get at them. And then, if they wanted to, they could ride off again and get clean away, because behind those high rocks there was plenty of ways for them to ease off into the back country.

But here we had what had been wanted for a long time but couldn't be had: a rustler, if he was a rustler, in our hands and not seen scooting off at the heels of a bunch of the cows which him and his pals had stampeded. That was the way that they was usually seen. But as for *catching* a real live rustler, it hadn't been done since Noah was a kid, so far as that range was concerned.

We went back and collected our yegg just as he was sitting up and beginning to hold his head and cuss. He had a lump the size of an egg on the back of his head, where he had landed on the rocks, and he kept feeling that lump with very tender fingers, and then damning us in fancy Spanish. He begins to tell Randal that he would pay for that day's work, and Randal looked like he *expected* to pay. So I grabbed the greaser and yanked him to his feet.

"Now kid," says I, "you leave off the Spanish and come to time with some English."

"Yo no sabe—" he begins.

"You lie!" says I. "I talk Spanish, too, but I can see by the look of the whites of your eyes that you're a Yank, kid, and Yank talk I'm gunna have out of you!"

At that, he spat out of the side of his mouth and shrugged his shoulders, as much as to say that he'd see me damned, but he wouldn't say a word.

So I says: "We'll give this gent a running chance. Frisk him, Rusty!"

Rusty frisked him. What he got was a pair of Colts, and a little mean two-barreled derringer strung on a horse-hair string around his neck, besides a big case-knife. Regular arsenal, that bird was.

"Now," says I to Rusty, "you get rid of all your guns and knives."

He done it, and he shelled out about as much as the yegg.

"Now," says I to the yegg, "you get ten yards start for the rocks. If you get to them, you'll be free, but if this fellow stops you and brings you back, you'll agree to tell us what you got on your chest. Is that fair?"

He give a look at Rusty, and it was easy to see that by the size of Rusty he didn't think that the big boy had much speed. Besides, except when Rusty was excited, he looked usually sort of sleek and lazy and contented with doing nothing. "All right," says the stranger. "I'll take on that chance!"

He got his ten yards start and away he went kiting, with Rusty after him. Well, it was a beautiful thing to see how the stranger flew for the rocks, but it was a lot beautifuller to see Rusty running in true sprinting style, with a nice high knee-action. He ran like a trotting hoss, and he nabbed his man inside of seventy-five yards. The thug meant fight and he tried to rough-house Rusty. But that just was to make us laugh. Rusty tied him in a figure eight and brought him back limp.

We all felt pretty good. I put the stranger down on a rock and told him to talk.

"Why the hell should I talk?" says he. "If you take me in, I charge you with assault with intent to kill. You got nothing on me, and all you'll buy will be a term in jail."

"Kid," says I, "that's a pretty good bluff, but once you get to a jail, they'll take a look at the Rogue's Gallery and they'll find the place in it where you used to fit."

He wilted a little at that and give me one of those nasty ratty side-looks that will live in the back corners of your mind for a long time, and wake you up in the middle of the night, remembering. But then he said, "All right. You take me in. I'm not gunna talk none!"

I says to Shorty: "Have you got any ideas, Shorty?"

Shorty grinned. He was a bad *hombre,* was Shorty.

"All right," says I. "Just take him out of sight, because I don't want Pepillo to see nothing nasty."

Have I forgot to tell you that Pepillo was along? What I mean to say is that he was *always* along, and never stayed ten seconds away from me, because he was always afraid that if he got around the corner from me, those big hands of Shorty would be clamped on him. There was Pepillo, sitting on a rock smoking one of his cigarettes with his sombrero pushed onto the back of his head. He was a little thinner and a little browner from the riding that he had been doing. But otherwise he was fit and as sassy as ever. Which was a wonder. But he had a great way with a hoss. Gave it a free hand, like a woman riding, and since he never fought his hoss, the hoss never fought him. He was always playing along having a good time, while the rest of us was working hard in the saddle.

"Do not mind me, señor," says Pepillo. "Only—that man is not a Mexican. He has broken his word, and Mexicans never do that!"

The boys give him a laugh, but Pepillo shrugged his shoulders. Just then, his smile was wiped out and he turned grey. Off yonder, where Shorty had taken his man, there was a yell. Not a yell, either—it was a scream.

I started head first for the place, but before I got there, here was Shorty leading his man back to us. What Shorty had done, I don't know, but he still had his damned mean grin on his face, and the crook was as limp as a rag. He didn't have any spirit of independence left in him—not none to speak about.

He sat right down where I had put him in the first place, and he talked like a little boy reading a lesson out of a book. If he ever stopped for a minute, I only had to jerk a thumb towards Shorty, and that would loosen up his tongue again.

What he told us was a facer. He said that Almadares, after making his clean-up on the range, had gone to that Valentin Mauricio and asked for his niece, Leonor, which had been arranged for, beforehand. And Mauricio was very agreeable about it, but when they went to get the girl, she was gone!

Mauricio swore that he didn't know anything about her disappearance. Almadares swore that that was a lie, and that the fact was that Mauricio must of sent the girl away on purpose to beat Almadares out of what was coming to him by rights. It was a grand mix-up.

"Look here," I busted in. "This here Almadares is a sort of a perfect man, ain't he, handsome and young and all that?"

"There is only one Almadares," says this gent, with a swagger of his head. "There is only one!"

"Well," says I, "then he must be right and Mauricio lied, eh? No girl would turn down an Almadares!"

"Not if she had good sense," says the crook, "but Valentin's niece ain't so very straight in the head, they say. She's got a kind of a crazy way about her, and you never know where she's gunna jump the next second!"

"All right," says I, "but go on."

He went on, all right. There was a grand bust between the two big rustlers. Mauricio got his men together, and because he knew that he was going to have a battle ahead, he tried to steal a march by surprising Almadares, in the middle of the night. He *did* surprise Almadares, too, but though he waded through some of the men of Almadares, he didn't get to Almadares himself, and that devil got the last of his men together and went through the Mauricios like a hot knife through butter.

The Mauricio gang headed for the tall timber, and they got to it, but while their backs was against the wall, Almadares just posted his men all around the spot, and he sat down to a siege.

That was a good many days ago. In the meantime, Almadares and his men ran out of provisions, in spite of what they could shoot, close and handy, and that was why this crook and the other pair had come down— to fetch off a few of the Randal cows to fill the pot.

"And if Almadares and his crew is hungry," says I, "I suppose that old Mauricio and his lot are about starved?"

"They are boiling leather and chewing it!" said that rat of a man—and it made my stomach shrink up into a knot to think of such hunger as that!

CHAPTER XIX

You will see the idea that popped into my head. You'll see it just as quick as I did.

I says to the informer: "How many men has old Mauricio?"

"About twenty-two," says he.

"And how many has Almadares?"

"Seventeen, now that I'm gone."

"Eh? Seventeen keeping twenty-two bottled up?"

"You forget, señor. One of the seventeen is that Pablo Almadares, and he is the same as ten."

Mind you, this wasn't any Mexican getting enthusiastic about Almadares. It was a Yank, the same as you or me. And there was no doubt that he meant what he said. He simply rolled his eyes when he talked about his boss.

Well, altogether, counting the party of Almadares and the party of Mauricio, there was not more than forty men up there in the mountains. Counting Randal and myself, there was eleven of us on this party—and eleven looks pretty small beside of forty. However, if I went back to the ranch and drummed up everybody that was able to shoot straight, I could bring out a party of sixteen, not counting Randal and me, which made it eighteen.

Now, with eighteen men well armed and prepared for their work; well rested and ready to hit hard and fast; something ought to be done. I says to the stranger:

"Kid, what's your name?"

"Chisholm," says he.

"You lie," says I. "Now, you let me have the straight of it."

"So help me God!" says he.

"God ain't no help to you," says I. "Not this far away from town. You come through with the facts. And you can't deceive me; I know too much about you already."

"All right," snarls the kid. "You guys are too much for me. I'll tell you. My name is Chet Roscoe."

He said it the way he might mean it, with his teeth set and his eyes glaring at me, as if he dared me to accuse him of all the crimes that he might of committed under that name, but when I looked at him again and nodded, it seemed to me that a sort of a look of relief come into his eyes.

I yanked a Colt out of its holster and I jammed it under the nose of this fellow.

"You skunk!" says I. "Lemme hear your name!"

He was so mad that he almost bit at the muzzle of the gun, and he shrank back and licked the blood from his lips, because I'd been a little stronger than necessary with the handling of that gat. And there he crouched and cringed, enough to make your stomach sick, and he looked at me and he started to speak; and he looked at the others and he shrank again. Then he beckoned me and I leaned over close to him.

"I'm Sammy Dance," says he. "For God's sake don't let nobody know!"

Well, I'd never heard of any Sammy Dance, but I knew that it must be the name of a gent that had done something pretty low as well as bad. A mere killer don't have to hide his head on the range, but when a man has killed some old man or a woman, then things are bad for him west of the Rockies. And I aimed to guess that this Sammy Dance must of done some such thing. I stepped back from him full of disgust, but I needed him too bad to be too mean to him.

I says: "Sammy, will you lead us up there where Almadares and old Mauricio are fighting it out?"

He put up both hands as though I was trying to hit him. He says: "For God's sake, mister, have a heart! Almadares would never rest till he got me!"

"Almadares won't have a chance," says I. "Because we're gunna scoop the whole lot of them in."

He started to shake his head, but I didn't have time to argue the case with him.

I started the boys back towards the ranch-house, and on the way I told them what I expected of them. It would of been one thing to take them right up through the mountains and tell them what I wanted after I got them there, but they wasn't the kind that had to be handled with gloves. They was all men, and the manlier that you treated them, the better that they would respond to the treatment. As we rode along, I told them everything that I hoped to do, the same as if they was lieutenants, and had to lead a lot of men apiece, instead of having to lead only themselves. I told them that I expected to leave the ranch about three in the morning of the next day with all of our men loaded down with our best guns. That we would ride along for the foot of the mountains, and that there we would change ourselves and our saddles to the backs of our best hosses; the same ones that we was riding now. Then we would sneak up through the mountains, with Sammy Dance to show us the way, and we would surprise that Almadares and his crew, and scoop them in, and while Mauricio and his gang was thinking that we was reinforcements, and helping us on the other side to clean up Almadares, then we would turn around and smear Mauricio all over the face of the map.

Maybe that sounds like a pretty ambitious sort of a program and no doubt in the world but that it was, but all the same, I was pretty sure that it would work. While we tackled Almadares, we would have the other gang of greasers working for us, and that would actually put the odds in our favor. And after we polished them off, we would be able to deal with Valentin Mauricio pretty neat.

I talked this over with the boys, and Shorty didn't agree. He said that the minute that gringos showed up in the offing, there wouldn't be nothing to it. All of the greasers would throw in together and they would fight like devils. However, Shorty was for trying the thing. Even if the Mexicans all throwed together for the fighting of us, we would still have a pretty fair chance of beating the lot of them. The odds wouldn't be more than two to one, as Shorty pointed out, and we'd have the advantage of the surprise to work for us. Altogether, it looked good to him. So did it to big Rusty McArdle. Rusty had been chafing a mite during the last few days. He knowed that he wasn't showing up in the best light while all the work was riding range, and such. He was fair aching for a scrap, and this here mix-up that I promised the boys was so much to his liking that he was smiling to himself all the way back to the ranch-house, and once in a while you would hear a soft laughter. You would know that that come from Rusty!

The rest of the boys bucked up very well, too. They figured that it would be a serious scrap, but not one of them backed up a mite. And when I looked them over, I got more confident every minute. Oh, they was a sweet lot of lambs, they was! There would be a hot time for anybody that had the nerve to try to comb their wool. I tell you that no Alexander nor no Napoleon ever felt a mite more happier in his army than I did in mine!

When we got back to the house, I says to Randal was there any place where we could put Sammy Dance away where he couldn't get out, and he says that there is a perfect place in the cellar. I went down and looked at it, and there I found just what I wanted. It was mostly dug out of bedrock, that little room. It had a window about a foot square that no man could ever wriggle through, and it had a door that you couldn't knock down with a battering ram. So we turned Sammy loose in there. I put in a cot for him, fixed him up with some grub, and he took things comfortable with his cigarettes, so that you could see that it wasn't the first time that he had made himself at home in quarters where he couldn't leave without permission. After that, I locked the door, put the key in my vest pocket, and went up the stairs with Pepillo.

Says I to Pepillo: "Well, kid, how come that you ain't had much to say?"

"Why should I talk," says Pepillo, "when you're not willing to hear good advice?"

"Let's have it," says I, "and then I'll make up my mind for myself."

"It's only this," says Pepillo. "That you don't know that Almadares!"

"Do *you* know him?" says I.

"Sure," says the kid. "Don't I, though? And every

Mexican knows about him. He is like Achilles. He cannot lose a fight. That is his way!"

"He is gunna change his way now, though," said I. "These boys of mine mean mischief!"

Pepillo nodded.

"They will kill many men," says Pepillo. "But what good is that if the Almadares gets away? He will raise more men and come back to fight again, and the second time it will be *he* who makes the surprise attack!"

He was dead set on that fact. You couldn't budge him on it, so I stopped arguing.

We all turned in early, that night. The hosses was ready. The men would be on deck by three o'clock, and all was to be set. I seen to that, made my rounds at about ten, and then I went to bed. The last that I seen was Pepillo sitting up cross-legged on his goatskin rug. He blew the lamp out and still he sat there, and I watched the glow and the darkening of the end of his cigarette until I went to sleep.

I waked up with a queer feeling that somebody was leaning over my bed. I reached out and quick and grabbed an arm so soft that the grip of my fingers went right to the bone, and I heard Pepillo gasp: "Mercy, in God's name, señor! You will break my arm!"

And something clinked on the floor. I jumped up and, dragging Pepillo along with me, I lighted the lamp. I seen that Pepillo was so scared that he was white. He was so scared that he didn't have any words on tap.

Then I went back with the lamp and I seen what had dropped from his hand when I grabbed him. It was lying there on the floor as big as life—the key to the cellar room where I had locked up Sammy Dance in the afternoon of the day before!

CHAPTER XX

I looked at the key and then at the kid. What had the damn little Blue Jay been up to now, in the way of mischief? I asked him, but he scowled at me and wouldn't speak.

"If you've been raising some kind of hell, kid, and messing up with this plan of mine," I says to the Blue Jay, "I'll give you such a hiding that you'll never forget it. Y'understand?"

And I picked up my quirt and took a hard grip on it. He simply swallered hard, but he wouldn't speak, and so I went down into the cellar, still dragging the kid along with me.

I opened the door with the key and looked inside. There was no sign of Sammy Dance!

Well, when I had finished lighting the little lamp that was down there, I closed the door and set down. I was so sick to find Dance gone that I was weak.

"Blue Jay," says I to Pepillo, "will you tell me now why you done it?"

He shook his head.

"Look here," says I. "This was the biggest chance that I'll ever have in my life. I could of blotted out that gang of thugs. I could of made rustling the most unpopular sport in the world, so far as the Sour Creek Valley is concerned, and here you've spoiled my game for me. You've turned that yegg loose. Damn your heart, will you tell me why you done it?"

At that, some of the color jerked back into his face. "I shall tell you nothing under compulsion," says he. Well, when I thought how he had ruined everything, and how Sammy Dance was scooting back through the night to get to Almadares ahead of us and tell Almadares everything that we planned on, I simply couldn't stand it any longer. I took both of the slim wrists of the kid in the fingers of my left hand.

"Blue Jay," says I to him, "I've stood a hell of a lot from you, and so has other folks. I like the nerve that you got, and the quick wits that you got. But one thing that you need mighty bad is a dad to lick you into shape. Now, kid, I'm so hot that I could bust you into pieces and welcome, but I ain't gunna. All that I'm gunna do is to give you the beating that you need. I'm gunna give you a dressing down that will serve you for a long time!"

He jumped back from me, but it wasn't any good. There was enough strength in my one hand to bust the bones of both of his wrists, if I had wanted to turn on the pressure.

"Señor," says the Blue Jay. "Do not do it!"

"Bah!" says I. "Are you gunna beg off?"

At that, he leaned over quick and sank his teeth in my wrist. The pain and the surprise made me let go and he jumped for the door. He was almost through it when I caught the nape of his neck and yanked him back. Then I picked him up by the wrists again. I was so mad that there was blackness before my eyes.

I says: "Pepillo, I swear that I'm prayin' to God to keep me from doing anything wrong, but you've got this coming to you!"—And I cut him across the shoulders with that quirt.

He didn't yell and he didn't wriggle any more. The minute that he felt that lash bite home, he stood stiff and straight and just looked at me. I let the quirt hang in the air for half a second, and he says:

"Señor, it was to keep you from running your head into sure death that I turned him loose."

"Sure death?" says I.

"Almadares!" says Pepillo. "I tell you that you would be no more to him than I would be to you! Than I am now, in your hands!"

He said it like he meant it, too, but just then the suggestion that I would of been helpless in the hands of another man didn't make any great winning with me. It sent the blackness swimming across my eyes again, and I slashed home half a dozen cutting blows, hitting, without no aim at all.

Then what brought me back to my senses was the fact that he wasn't yelling, and he wasn't trying to get away, and he wasn't tugging at my wrists none. That wasn't like a boy. He ought to of been screaming, the way that I had laid that quirt into him; and a quirt is the most cuttingest thing that there is, next to a knife. Only it hurts a lot worse than any knife ever done!

The quietness of the kid, as I was saying, it brought me to my sense, and the blackness cleared away from before my eyes, and there I seen Pepillo standing with his head up and turned a little away from me, as though he didn't want to see my face, and in his eyes, there wasn't any pain—only a terrible great shame.

The quirt dropped right out of my hand. I turned his wrists loose. Those wrists, they was white as snow from the force that had been gripping them.

I don't know why I should of felt the way that I did. The kid had been bad, and real bad. I leave it to you, didn't he deserve a licking—and a hard licking?

But well, a quirt is a hoss-whip—and the skin of Pepillo was pretty thin! And besides, hitting at him, blind with rage, an end of the lash just flicked across his face and left a white mark that was turning red and raising in a little weal. It wasn't a bad mark, y'understand, but somehow the fact that I had hit the kid in the face was like a knife drove into my heart.

When he seen that I had turned him loose, he turned around to the door. But I jumped in front of him. Well, it was grand to see him step back and look me in the eye.

"Is there more, señor?" says he. "Because I shall not attempt to run away."

"Pepillo," says I, "I didn't understand—"

The kid sunk down on the cot of Sammy Dance and he sat there with his eyes closed.

"Ah, Dios, Dios, Dios!" says Pepillo, and he laid a hand against his throat as though he was stifling.

It was no play acting. You would think by the look of him that I had just finished hoss-whipping a cross between a Duke of York and a United States senator.

"I dunno how it is," I had to tell the kid. "But I'm sick. I've done wrong. I shouldn't of used a quirt. And

—except I was so blind mad—wouldn't of hit you in the face. I want to ask you to believe me that I wouldn't mean to hit you in the face—with a whip or anything, son!"

"Son?" says Pepillo, and he looked up at me with a queer little laugh. "Ah, well," says he, "if you have finishing beating me, with the whip, spare me from your clumsy tongue, señor. May I go?"

I held the door for a minute. I wanted a lot to find something else to say, which something else seemed to be needed, but I couldn't discover a thing. Only I knew that I was sick.

"You're gunna leave me, Pepillo?" says I.

He steps right out past me and turns around to stare, when he hears me say that.

"Is it likely that I should stay?" says he.

"Is ain't likely, son," says I, "only if you would try to listen to me for a minute, maybe I could explain why it would be for your own good!"

There was a sort of spasm that crossed his face and ten thousand devils shone in his eyes.

"Do you think that I don't detest you more than there are words to tell it?" says he. "You dog of a gringo. You *dog* of a gringo!" And doggone me, if he didn't bust out crying. Yes, sir, all my whipping hadn't raised a tear to his eyes, but when he got so mad and so ashamed, that was the way that emotion turned loose in him!

I didn't try to comfort him. I just stood back and hung my head like a dog that had been kicked—and that was the only way that I could explain the way that I felt.

"Blue Jay," says I, "I don't mind all of your hard talk. I would only wish that you could find more harder words so that you could take it all out on me like that."

Then an idea come *bang!* right into my head. I grabbed up the quirt.

"Ah," said Pepillo, "is it to come again?"

I give him the handle of the whip.

"I sure acted like a low-down skunk to you, kid," says I. "Now I got a lot tougher hide and a lot stronger head than you got, but you're free to use that quirt on me till your arm aches with the weight of it. Go ahead and turn loose.

"You lie!" says Pepillo, shaking away his tears and

grinding his teeth at me in his awful rage. "You lie. You bluff! You know that I dare not!"

I took off my coat.

"Now," says I, "you go ahead, and see if I budge!"

"Then——" yells Pepillo.

He took the handle of that quirt with both hands and swung it around his head.

"Z-Zing!" it cut through the air, and slashed me across the breast. I cussed. I couldn't help it, because it hurt so bad, but I didn't budge, and I looked him in the eye.

He swung that quirt back again over his head, but when he seen me standing for the whip still, the fierceness, it appeared to run right out of his face. He drops the whip and gives a sob, and he turns and runs down the hall and then up the cellar stairs, his feet just flying.

"Pepillo!" I calls to him.

But the door upstairs, it slammed, and the echo was the only answer that I got. Pepillo was gone; I sure would never see him again. And on the way up from that cellar, I tell you that I was like a mourner at a funeral. Just that! And from the first minute that I see him in front of Gregorio's store in Sour City, to the last instant that he stood there with the quirt over his head, every picture of him come jump, right through my head.

It wasn't like losing a mere kid. When my old man died, and when my mother died, too—well, there was almost the same sort of sadness in losing of Pepillo; and even more, I'm ashamed to say. You try to explain it if you can. I couldn't, then!

I went on out to the bunkhouse and I waked up Shorty and Rusty McArdle. And you can believe me that they was both sleeping light.

I took them out into the pale of the moonlight and I says: "That gent that was gunna guide us is gone. The kid thought that we would get ourselves busted up a lot if we run into Almadares and his gang; and he stole the key from me and turned him loose!"

Rusty couldn't talk. He had been hankering for that fight so bad that he was fair thirsty for it, and now he was dumb. But Shorty could talk. The first minute or two couldn't be put down in print, what he said. After that: "I knew that the damned little rat would do us a harm before he got through!" says Shorty. "And when I get my hands on him, now—now, damn my eyes, if that ain't him sneaking away from the house, right now!"

It was. Across the moonlight, between the house and the barn, we had a glimpse of Pepillo walking through a gap in the trees. Well, I wanted to go after him and try to keep him back, but I didn't budge, because I knew that it would be useless. But when Shorty seen the kid, he let out a sort of a howl, like a wolf, and he lit out for him.

CHAPTER XXI

Well, the kid spotted that yell of Shorty's, and he turned
and tried to head back towards the house, but after he
had gone half a dozen jumps through that pale, misty
moonshine, he seen that he could never make the house,
because Shorty was running wonderful fast, just throwing himself across the ground and seeming to touch it
with his dangling hands, monkey-like.

Pepillo turned around and struck back through the
trees towards the barns, where he'd been headed when
I first seen him, but that false move and the change
of direction, it lost him a terrible lot of ground and
brought Shorty almost up to him.

They shot away, with the kid seeming to be almost
in the hands of Shorty half a dozen times, but still he
would dodge away around a tree and escape again. But
just as they went around the corner of the first shed, I
could see Shorty run right over Pepillo and scoop him up
off the ground—and the scream of Pepillo, it come tin-
gling and ringing in my ears and making my heart to
jump, very queer.

Then there wasn't any sound. What was happening
behind that there barn, there wasn't any token of. Just
the silence, which was harder to bear than yelling. I
tried to figure Pepillo taking the hammering of those big
hands of Shorty's without crying out; but the only picture
that would fit was of the Blue Jay lying on the ground,
and the thumbs of Shorty gripped into the hollow of his
throat, and shaking his head with its long black hair, up
and down. That picture would explain everything; and it
was about the only thing that would explain the silence.

121

I says: "By God, I think that Shorty is killing him."

"I hope he does!" says Rusty through his teeth. "I hope he enjoys the job, too, and I only wish that I was there to help him."

And with that he turns around and strides off into the bunkhouse. But when I see all of this, I made up my mind that I would have to get up there to the spot in time to help Pepillo a little, if I wasn't too late.

You'd think it hardly possible that Shorty would really try to kill the Blue Jay, but I knew how delicate Pepillo was under all of his sassiness, and the others didn't. And I seen that the only way to really handle him was to handle him gentle!

I made time, I can tell you, between the bunkhouse and the corner of the shed, but when I come closer, I hear the voice of Shorty break out into a sort of a wail:

"My God, my God, how could I of knowed?"

It stopped me like a punch in the face. He'd killed the kid, then; and he was saying that he didn't guess that Pepillo could possibly die so easy?

I took out my Colt. One thing was sure. If Pepillo was dead, Shorty should die beside him. No, I would do it with my hands. I put up that gun and I sneaked a few steps forward towards the corner of the barn.

Suddenly the voice of Pepillo answered Shorty, panting.

"Now that you know, you'll keep quiet about it, Shorty?"

"Ah," says Shorty. "I sure will. I'll never open my mouth, if you don't want me to!"

First, my heart swelled up to twice its normal size, I was so tickled to hear the kid speaking, and to know that he wasn't bad hurt. And then I was pretty near paralyzed with astonishment to hear the way that Shorty was talking. Who could this runt of a kid be, that knowing him made Shorty act like he had touched holy fire?

Ah that's just how he was acting, because when I come into the view of them around the corner of the shed, and crouched there, spying them out, I give you my eternal word that I seen Shorty standing first on one foot and then on the other foot, and holding his hat in his hand, with his head bare and his long, rough hair bristling in the night wind. A damn queer picture. I could of laughed my head off if I hadn't been so curious and so baffled.

Who was Pepillo, really? I didn't know that there was any royal family in the world that could make Shorty so filled with awe and with wonder as he seemed to be, now.

"I would ask you believe something," says Shorty —and I swear to you that his voice was shaking a good deal—"if I had guessed who you was, I would rather of cut off my right hand than to ever of touched you!"

"I believe you," says Pepillo.

"Here," says Shorty, "will you lemme brush you off?"

"Thank you," says Pepillo.

Well, there was Shorty actually getting down on his knees all the better to dust off that kid!

Maybe I haven't been able to give you the right idea about Shorty, but I tell you that I stood there and wouldn't believe what I was seeing with my own eyes. Because he was rough, that Shorty. He was about as rough as they make 'em. But I seen what I seen and I heard what I heard!

Only I think that what beat me most of all was the easy, careless way that the kid accepted the attentions that Shorty was giving him. Accepting him as though he was used to such attentions, and as though he was born with a right to them from any man; instead of being just a little vagrant guttersnipe the way that I had found him.

Shorty stood up and he backed away a little, like he wouldn't want to force himself on Pepillo too close. Then he seen something that made him start. He pointed to the face of the kid.

"Excuse me," says Shorty. "Did I do that?"

"No—it was Big Boy," says the Blue Jay.

"By God!" busts out Shorty. "A whip!"

Pepillo nodded.

"I'll fix him for that!" says Shorty, and doggone me if he didn't yank out his big black Colt and swing around and start away. He meant to murder me, and that was all that there was about it! Pepillo got in front of him in two jumps.

"You mustn't harm him!" says Pepillo. "I deserved it, after all—I think!"

"You—deserved it?" groans Shorty.

"I spoiled all of his plans."

"Damn him and his plans too!" says Shorty. "All that I want is just a minute alone with him—to sort of explain my views of what I think about him. Would you let me do that, please?"

"No," says Pepillo, "not for an instant. Promise me that you won't harm him!"

Yes, sir, I tell you that there stood Pepillo in front of Shorty and raised his hand a little, like he was the Pope, or something, and doggone me if Shorty didn't act like a good Catholic and back right up. Yes, he put away that revolver as meek as a lamb.

He says: "I got no right to touch him if you don't want me to."

"I want your promise," says Pepillo, a little impatient.

Shorty sort of gagged and swallowed.

"I promise!" he whispers.

"Thank you," says Pepillo, and he smiled on Shorty like that smile was enough reward for him, or for any man.

"I would like it," says Shorty, "if you could explain how might I be of any use to you? Actin' the way that I've done, most likely you write me down for a swine—which maybe I am, mostly. But I ain't forgot that I was born into a decent family in old England, and I would like to do a decent thing now, if you would tell me how. If you was planning to leave this here place and this here rat—this Big Boy—"

Pepillo shook his head and frowned a little.

"You mustn't speak that way of him," says he.

Doggone me, if Shorty didn't even swaller that.

"All right," says he, "only what I meant to offer was that if you might want a hoss for leaving on, I would be plumb tickled if you was to take my pinto hoss—"

It staggered me! That pinto was nearer to the heart of Shorty than any child to the heart of his pa. But here he was, offering that hoss to a kid that didn't stand kneehigh to a grasshopper.

"I can't take it from you, Shorty," says the kid. "Because—well, because I think that I'll go back to him, after all!"

"To Big Boy?" says Shorty, naming me with a lot of

effort, like I was a kind of a poison, or a snake, or something.

"Yes," says the Blue Jay.

Shorty throws out his arms and he groans:

"Don't you do it! Doggone me if I could stand to see you standing around—like a servant—and him—"

He choked, and couldn't say no more; but his fingers worked, and it wasn't hard for me to guess that where he wanted to plant them hands of his was in my throat.

"It's no use," says Pepillo. "I think that I shall have to stay."

And at that, Shorty didn't argue no more, but his head dropped forward, and looked as if he'd just heard about the death of his whole doggone family by shipwreck or something.

"I got no right to say nothing," says Shorty very sober. "You are the boss."

Now, by this time, I had had sure enough. And I backed away from the place where I had been seeing and hearing all of the funny things that had been happening. And I went off and walked by myself.

A little while earlier, it had seemed to me that nothing in the world mattered, really, except that I had lost my first chance to squelch the rustlers on the Sour Creek Valley. And then here I was forgetting all about Mauricio and the Pablo Almadares, and my deal with Randal, and my hope of the ranch, and all of that. All that I was thinking of, now, was that this here kid had hypnotized Shorty.

Ay, and he had sort of hypnotized me, too, as you've had a chance to see.

But that was different. It was plain that when Shorty scooped the kid off the ground, Pepillo must of said one word that stopped Shorty. What that one word or phrase must of been, I dunno. But there was a clue for me to follow up, as they say about the detectives—I'll tell you what the clue was.

I had always figgered that this here Shorty, he was the sort of a gent that was raised and growed altogether on the range, but here I had listened in on him saying that he had been born in England.

Now, why should he of throwed that in—and that remark about "good old" England, if it hadn't had some relation to Pepillo? The idea busted in my brain like a shooting star going to pieces in the middle of the air.

This here Pepillo, that I had ordered and thrown and kicked and whipped around, was really somebody terrible, terrible high up in the world over yonder in England. Somebody very near to the top, in fact! And the more that I pondered on that there thing, the more clear it was that I seen the truth about it.

He was so high that the thought that I had laid a whip onto the kid made Shorty want to murder me; so high that the knowing that he, Shorty, had laid hands on the kid, made Shorty almost want to take poison himself— and go so far that he would offer to give away his best cutting hoss!

Well, what would do that? It was easy to see a damn good reason. Those Englishmen are a pretty good lot, you take them for fighting or playing square, or doing anything that comes right and natural amongst men, but they got their funny places. Like who would be bothered, these days, with the having of a king. And would you say "my lord" to somebody? No, you wouldn't, nor would I. But these here Englishmen, they would, and they sort of like it, too, strange though that may seem—and damned strange, too!

I have had it from gents that of been there, that an Englishman he don't think nothing of taking off his hat, not only to this doggone king, but even to some duke or other, or even to a earl, maybe; which earls and such is terrible thick, over there, like millionaires with us, you know. But an Englishman, he don't care. You would think that he didn't have no pride at all, was you to see him standing in the rain to let some doggone earl that never done nothing go by him.

But here was the secret with Shorty, right enough. This kid he was high, mighty high. And here was me, an ornery low-down cowpuncher that had been ordering him around right and left—and actually laying a whip on his shoulders!

Well, I didn't like it, much. I liked it lot less than you would maybe guess. I went back towards the house feeling blue, and low, and meaner than nails in your shoe.

CHAPTER XXII

Sitting and thinking don't never do no good at a time like that, but I was bothered by a lot of little things, such as how could Pepillo have the kind of skin and eyes and lingo that he had and be a noble of England? But still, that could be explained pretty easy and logical, because you know how those high-faluting earls and princes and what not will marry around into foreign countries, simply disgusting.

You take a young count or something. Would he be contented to marry Sally Smith, pretty as a picture, straight as a string, and living right in the same block with him, that he went to school with, as you might say? No, he would not! which he would sooner go across to France or somewhere and he would pick up with some skinny French girl that didn't have no home training at all, and he would marry her and think that he was doggone smart to bring home a package of trouble like that.

But you folks know all of these things pretty near as good as I could. You could read 'em in the papers almost any day. So it was pretty plain that the pa of Pepillo— you couldn't write him down much smaller than a duke, at the least—he must of married out into another country and maybe that marriage wasn't none too happy. He married some Spanisher, say; and that was how come that Pepillo knowed so much Spanish lingo as well as English so good.

Well, most likely there was a good deal of trouble around the house; because you never could tell when a foreigner woman like that would start carryings on with the nearest handy man—the butler, say, or even the gardener—and maybe it made the old Duke pretty mean, and he might of started to take some of his meanness out on Pepillo. Which you can see that being what he was, Pepillo wouldn't take nothing from nobody, and so he up and left the old man and the wife flat and started out on his own—and that was how that I found him.

You can see that this reasoning is pretty straight, and if you go back over it, it would be pretty hard for you to pick out any flaw in it, I suppose. Anyway, by the time that I had worked out these here things satisfactory, the door of my room opens soft and there is Pepillo.

He says: "Well, I'm over my mad. I'm taking my licking and coming back, if it's the same to you, old timer."

Well, how would you feel, if you was to have a young duke come along like that and step into your room? I jumped up quick and got a little red.

"Sit down, and welcome, your honor," says I.

"How do you get that way," says Pepillo, "and what'ye mean by 'your honor'? Are you kidding me?"

I seen that he didn't want to bust through his incognito none, and was it up to me to force his hand? I should say not! I says: "All right, Pepillo. If you want it that way, I suppose it's your right. I'll treat you any way that you say, because you sure got a lot coming from me!"

Pepillo sat down cross-legged on a chair and dropped his chin on his fist.

"What's biting you?" says Pepillo. "You act like a fish out of water."

"Why," said I, "as a matter of fact, there's nothing wrong with me, only—" I could feel myself getting hotter and hotter.

"Go on," says Pepillo, scowling at me. "What's under your hat?"

I just stammered and stared.

"You're blushing!" says Pepillo. Then all at once he jumped up, pretty red, himself.

"Big Boy!" says he, and points his finger at me. "You were behind the corner of that shed!"

I couldn't lie out of it, though I would of liked to.

I says: "Son, I don't want to embarrass you none. You got your own reasons, but if I was you, I would go back to your family."

Pepillo, he gives me a long, long look that had me shifting from one foot to the other.

"Just what d'you know?" says he.

"That Shorty wants to murder me," says I.

"And why?" says he.

"Why—you know, Pepillo."

"Maybe I do," says he, "but I want *you* to say it!"

"I didn't hear everything," says I. "Only, it's plain to make out that you must of come from some pretty high up family, Pepillo. I ain't pressing you for no more information than you feel like handing out. Your business is your own. I know that! What your old man is, I dunno, or why you left him, but these here earls and dukes and things, they got troubles of their own, I know."

"Earls and dukes?" says Pepillo, frowning at me. And then he grinned. He sat down again and he took a long breath.

"Look here," says I, "if maybe you're lacking for the funds to take you back to him—"

Pepillo shook his head.

"I'm never going back," says he, "so stop worrying about that. As for the rest, so far as you're concerned, I'm Pepillo, or the Blue Jay, or any other silly name that you choose to call me. Does that go, Big Boy?"

"Sure," says I. "Only, I feel sort of foolish about—"

Pepillo began to laugh to himself, with his eyes dancing.

"What's wrong?" says I.

" 'Your honor!' " says Pepillo, and then he begins to laugh again, and he laughed so hard that he had to wrap his arms around himself and rock back and forth in the chair and fair shout. I had to start grinning myself.

"Look here, you monkey," says I, "I'm standing a good deal. Don't you forget—"

"The whip?" says Pepillo.

It brought me up with a start, I can tell you, like there was a curb bit in my teeth. But Pepillo, he slips out of his chair and he comes over to me.

"I'm not going to explain about myself," says he, "but I'll tell you this: I'm no better than you used to think me. I'm only worse, a lot!"

He stuck out his hand, and I took it like it was ginger-bread.

"As for the whipping: now that it's over, I have to admit that I deserved it. Maybe it will do me good. I don't bear you any malice, Big Boy. We're quits all around, if you balance that against me turning Sammy Dance loose—"

"Sammy Dance?" I yelled at him. "Why, how did you come to know that name?"

"Why, you told me. Was it a slip?" says he. But his eyes had wobbled a little bit to the side from mine, and I knew that he was lying.

"Pepillo," says I, "that's a lie and a loud one! Excuse me for saying so!"

"It's a fact," says Pepillo.

Well, I let it go at that; but I knew that I hadn't used the name of Sammy Dance to anybody. Then how did it come that the kid knew his name? The more that I thought about it, the more it beat me. I could see that there was oceans more to this kid than I had been able to guess, and I made up my mind that I would simply lie low and keep my eyes and my ears open for a while, and then, maybe I would get on the right track, after all.

Pepillo, he went to the other side of the room, and he begun to do some of his chores, because the sun was near rising, and the day was beginning. He fetched out a pair of my old boots, and begun to oil them up.

"What are you laughing at?" says I, pretty soon.

"Nothing, your honor!" says he.

Well, I fetched a lick at him, but he dodged me, and I went on down to see how the air was below.

I fetched into Randal, pretty soon. He had heard the news. He says: "What're you gunna do to that brat, Big Boy?"

"Leave him be," says I. It seemed a million years ago that I had been planning to ride against Almadares and the rest. "Tell me, Randal, how would folks speak to a duke?"

"Why, they would call him Your Grace, I suppose," says Randal.

That explained it! I damned myself pretty good. I knew that it was "your—" something or other, but I had missed my guess pretty far, as you can see for yourself. Anyway, I was glad that Pepillo and me was partly back on the old footing, and I went out for a walk in the fresh of the morning, while breakfast was getting ready.

When I went out, up the drive comes an old withered up gent on a mustang that was covered with sweat and dirt. Looked like he had been riding the whole night through. He jumps down, very spry.

"Look here, young man," says he, "just fetch my hoss around to the stable and give it a good feed of grain, will you?"

It took me back, a little. I never cuss an old man. I just said to this gent: "What hinders you from fetching your own hoss, stranger? I'm busy!"

He give me a sharp look.

"What are you busy at?" says he.

"Watching the sunrise," says I, and turns my back on him.

Just then the front door slammed and there was Randal, singing out: "Why, grandfather, where did you drop from?"

"I dropped from that saddle," says the old man. "Why don't you hire men who'll obey orders, Harry? This fellow says that he won't feed my hoss!"

I turned around in a trance. Yes, sir, it was old Henry Randal. And it was plain that I hadn't boosted the stock of his grandson none. I took the hoss and went away, kicking the stones out of my path and damning the world at large.

CHAPTER XXIII

Out in the barn, I met up with Shorty and big Rusty Mc-Ardle. Rusty, he looked pretty sad, but he grinned and waved at me, but Shorty, he only glared when I said good morning to him.

"Hey, Shorty, what's eating you?" says Rusty. "Don't you see the Big Boy?"

"Damn the Big Boy, and you, too," says Shorty, and he went off to catch him a hoss for the day's work.

"What's up?" says Rusty to me.

"Rusty," says I, "there is so damn much in the air around this here ranch that's wrong, that I can't tell where to begin to talk about it. Besides, what I feel is mostly guesswork, and not many facts. But I'll tell you one thing, to put in your pipe and smoke. Old Henry Randal has just blowed in, and he'll start counting cows, to-day —and he's gunna find that the count is short."

I was right, too. When I got back to the house, I found that old man Randal was as chipper as you please. He chattered away all through the breakfast.

"Your men were running all over the house, the last time that I was here, Harry," says he. "How does it happen that they've stopped?"

"I got tired of it," says Harry, "and I put an end to it."

"*You* put a stop to it?" says the old man, and he looked up and blinked his eyes at his grandson like a hawk that sees a mouse under its pounce. "*You* put a stop to it!"

"Ay," says Harry, and he gives me a look, as much as to say, "Don't give me away!"

Of course, I wouldn't of said a word, because Harry's

game was my game. Harry's winning meant my winning, in the end.

Old Henry Randal, he went on with his breakfast, and his talking at the same time; which he was eating enough to keep any strong hired man going, and he was talking enough for two, at the same time. He wore his eighty years like they was thirty, and I couldn't help thinking what a power of a man he must of been when he was younger. I was wrong there, though. When he was a youngster, I found out later, he'd been a good deal of an invalid, but as he got older, all the sicknesses had died out of him and withered away, and left him just a sound, well-weathered old stick of a man.

He told us that he hadn't intended coming over for some days, but that he hadn't been able to sleep the night before, and so he got up, dressed, and went for a ride; and for lack of any better place to ride to, he had come to the Sour Creek ranch. Which was the last place that he was wanted, of course—but you could see that that didn't make any difference to him!

This was a snappy, cold morning, with the wind blowing straight down from the snows on the mountains, and pretty soon, old Randal says: "Let's have some fire here, Harry; let's have some fire here, man. D'you want to freeze my old blood in my body?"

Harry was pretty eager to please the old hawk, and he jumped up and touched a match to the fire that was laid on the hearth. In a moment, the flames were rising in sheets and columns and roaring up the chimney. It was a whale of a fireplace, that. When Stephen Randal set himself to build a house, he begun at the ground and dug out a cellar that would have served for a castle foundation, and then he went ahead and he built the rest of the old house to match it. The dining-room was a place where you could of put fifty men down the long table, and even with all of the centerboards out, that table couldn't be shrunk up to a handy size. The three of us—the old man, Randal and me—were sitting around it with yards of space between, and there had to be a nigger or two always handy to pass things around. But the fireplace was made to match the room. Even me, I could stand right up straight in it. It was like another room, and the irons was like bronze frames for a ten-ton truck. There was wood to fit with irons and a fireplace like that. If you was to throw in an armful of ordinary firewood, it would burn up like so much kindling and not send out so much as a glow across the rest of the room. What you needed was sections of a tree, just split across once or twice, and heaved into the fireplace.

"Put on some wood! Put on some wood!" says old Henry Randal, and he clapped his hands together. He was terrible impatient. Everything had to be done on the jump, to suit him, and when you got it done, his brain was already turning the corner and busy with something else in the distance. I never seen such a man to make other folks nervous.

The two niggers got the sign from their boss and they run over and took hold on a couple of the big chunks of wood and laid them on the fire, and they grunted and groaned as they heaved at them. It takes strength to handle heavy timber, but there's a knack to it, too: like handling baled hay, almost, but not quite so scientific as that.

"Look at 'em!" says old Henry Randal, pushing back his chair and slapping his hands together. "Why, when I was young, one boy could of handled wood like that; and bigger. I tell you, the world is going to the devil, and so are the men in it. Foreman—what's the name of your foreman, Harry?"

Harry Randal give me a sort of a desperate look. He didn't want my real name to leak out. He'd never give me any name on the ranch except "Smith," so now he says: "His name is Jim Smith."

"Smith, hey?" says the old man. "Seems to me like I've known somebody by the same name, before this. I can't recollect the face, though. Did you ever live in Kansas City? No? Well, Mr. Jones, will you let me see if you can handle that wood any better than the niggers can?"

I was a little mad. I got up and brushed the niggers away and picked up the wood and chucked it on the fire. It really was light, and if the niggers hadn't been in each other's way, they could of handled it like nothing at all, of course.

I started back towards the table, dusting my hands, while Harry Randal smiled and swaggered in his chair a little, exactly as though he had done the work himself.

"You see," says he, "that people haven't run down hill so far as you might think, grandfather!"

"You talk when your turn comes," snaps the old man, very sharp. "By the way, that fire has no backlog. Why don't you put in the backlog, Jones? Why don't you do your work properly, once you put your hand to it? If you're a foreman on a ranch, you've got to set an example of thoroughness to the other men. What sort of an example is such slipshod work as this? There's the backlog, Jones! Go put it on the fire, will you?"

I stopped and gave the old chap a look. He was old, but even so he made my hands itch, and a ten pound weight of words came boiling up in my throat. I had to shut my teeth with a click to hold them back, and so I turned around quick and put my back towards that old devil.

What he had pointed to for the backlog was a big round section of a scrub oak that had been brought into the house by mistake a couple of months before, as Randal had told me. In the first place, it should have been split. In the second place, it should have been allowed a whole year of drying out and seasoning before it was so much as split.

There it lay on the floor on a pair of boards. It was a darned big log, no matter what it was made of, but it happened to be made of oak, and that oak happened to be green. So, you take it by and large, the wood was about as heavy as iron. I knew it, and so would any one know it, by the look of the solid grain of the end of it. You could see where the teeth of the big saws had blunted on the hard fibre of that old tree, and how they had dulled and worked crooked, and just polished the wood instead of cutting through it. The tramp that cut through that tree would of earned a whole week's board.

And that was the elephant that old Randal wanted me to put in the fire as a backlog! Why, it weighed as much as a piano, and it had been such a job for the blockheads that had brought it in through the narrow doors from the outside, that it had been left lying near the fireplace all of this time. I looked at that whale of a stick sort of helpless and Harry jumped up.

"Let me give you a hand, Big Boy," says he.

"Sit down, sit down, sit down!" barks old Henry Randal at us. "Sit down, will you? And tell me if Jones has asked for any help? He's big enough to do the job alone, and I hope that he's not puppy enough to ask for help before he finds that the job has him beaten! I hope that he's not just made of putty!"

I tell you, that old chap had a devil hidden under his tongue, and every time he talked, the devil jumped up and showed his face!

I grabbed hold on the log and heaved, just blind with anger, but all that I managed was to give it a twist that made it roll a bit from side to side—and there was so much weight to it that it fair made the whole room quiver!

"He *is* beat, you see?" says the old devil, as I straightened up again and turned towards the table. "One effort: that's enough for him, and Jones is beat! Big, but soft; that's what he looks like to me!"

When you get very mad, it's like a red flame, but when you get still madder, you get a white flame instead. At first you could scream and yell and stamp and tear things, but when the full anger comes, then you can stand still and smile, and what you want to do then is to poison.

I gave one look to old Henry Randal, and Harry says: "Why, grandfather, it took four men—"

"Four fiddlesticks!" says old Henry Randal. "Don't tell me what a man and a man's work may be. Don't I know?"

"Very well," says Harry Randal, "but I'm afraid that you're expecting the impossible, sir!"

"Am I? Am I? Well—there he goes for a second try. I'm glad to see that your man Jones has a sense of shame, at the least!"

Well, you can't imagine anybody talking like that, but Henry Randal was old enough and mean enough to say everything that come into his head, and there was hardly anything but what would come into his head some time or other.

I laid hold on that log with such a grip that it hurt the ends of my fingers bad, and then I leaned back and sank my knees down, and got my arms straight, and my chest and my hips and the balls of my feet as much in a line as possible.

After that I began to straighten. It was astonishing to me, but that log raised under my hands. I felt muscles and tendons strain, and there was snapping sounds in my shoulders, but that log heaved up with me, and I dragged it back towards the fireplace.

"Hold up!" yelled Harry Randal. "You're scratching the floor to pieces—"

"Shut up, you idiot!" cries Henry Randal. "Will you shut up and leave him be? Damn the floor and the scratches!"

I got the log in front of the fire and there all at once I staggered, for my foot had caught in the floor—

"There he goes!" pipes out Henry Randal, clapping his hands together. "There he goes. Beaten right on the verge of success! Beaten and giving up right at the gate—"

I tell you, it fell on me like a whip. All that I would of liked to do to that old devil went into the strength of my hands and my arms and my shoulders; and I lifted that whole log in my arms and dropped it into the fire! It sent a crash of sparks and smoke up into my face, and the released weight made me stagger backwards.

I went numb all over. The blood rushed into my head until I thought that my temples would burst. And through a cloud that had settled across my eyes, I managed to find a chair and to drop into it. I tell you that a three year old child could have pushed me down at that minute, I was so weak. I felt, all over, the way an arm feels, when it has gone to sleep.

The rush of the sparks had sent a shower out upon the floor and Harry Randal, he jumped up with a yell, and swearing that the house would be sure to catch fire and burn down, he set about putting the sparks out. But old Henry Randal, you would of thought that he didn't give a damn whether the house burned or not. Rather, you would of said that he might of *preferred* for it to burn down.

When I come back to myself by little and little, there was young Randal pointing to the little black spots all over the floor, and to the way that the big log had squashed the life out of the fire, and clamoring about the big scratch in the floor. But that old grandfather of his sat with his chin in one withered claw of a hand and blinked his bird eyes like a bird, and never left off staring at me.

"I thought so!" says he at last. "Maybe you had a mite of help in handling the punchers, Harry? Maybe this Jones, or Smith, or whatever he might be, gave you a hand?"

Smart? I tell you that old rascal could see through about anything. And Harry Randal turned red, like a fool, and then he began to stammer something. But while he was telling the niggers to rush around and get the fire going again; and apologizing for the smoke that was rolling into the room; and getting himself into a general sweat, old Randal, he heaves himself up out of the chair and he says: "It's too damned hot to be staying indoors. Come along, Jones. You and me will take a ride around the place, to-day."

He went out and we got a hoss for him, and I took another, and without another word to Harry and without another word to any of the boys, he snaked me off with him for a tour of the ranch.

He was very brisk and very cheerful, now, and the way that he asked questions, you would of thought that he was my boss, and that Harry was just his hired man with no real interest in the place.

About noon we was a long distance away from the house and the old chap, he said: "Well, we'll make us a fire and have a lunch. What have you got to eat with you?"

I pulled out my saddle bag and there was hardtack, and a mite of bacon, and some cornmeal flour and a bit of salt in a sack, and some raisins, and a little package of tea. I always have a small snack of food like that along with me. You never can tell when it will come in handy. Two or three times I've had to make a hurry move across the hills, and when those times come along it pays to have some food along. If a lot of fellows are riding along behind you, they figure on you heading for the nearest town or the nearest shack to get chuck, but if you can support yourself in the open, you'll take a course that will fool them. At any rate, that's been my experience.

This Henry Randal, he looks into the bag and all he seemed to see was the bacon.

"Bacon!" he snarls. "Bacon! You expect me to eat salt meat, at my time of life? Bacon! I'll be damned if I ever heard of anything like it!"

I had to bear down hard to keep from exploding, but I want you to understand just what a mean, prying, overbearing sort of a gent he was. Then he sings out: "There's our fresh meat, Jones! Shoot that rabbit for me!"

By the time that I had been able to pull my revolver and turn around in the saddle, the jack-rabbit was a good long distance away. And I was glad of that. I had done absolutely no shooting on that range, and I didn't *intend* to do any, because I knew that before I had pulled the trigger half a dozen times, the whole gang would tumble to the fact that I was a dud, so far as guns was concerned.

But here was I with a revolver, and yonder was a jackrabbit, just about out of range, and jumping back and forth in a twisting course as it ran, scared to death, and its ears flagging back with its speed of running. Nobody is ever expected to hit a running rabbit with a revolver shot, no matter at what range. So there wouldn't be any disgrace that I could see in missing here.

So I just tipped the muzzle of that gun up, hip high, and shot without trying to take a bead. Well, the rabbit it jumped a mile into the air and I thanked God that luck had taken my shot near enough to scare it. The rabbit come down—and where it hit the ground it flattened out like a pancake!

Yes, sir, I took hold of myself with both hands, as you might say, I was so surprised, but I forced any expression of surprise out of my face. I wanted to keep those squinting, narrowing, drilling eyes of the old chap from boring into me any more, though, and so I touched up my hoss with the spurs and rode right over to pick up my kill. And of all the shooting that I ever done, the killing of that rabbit was the only shot that I could ever call good.

CHAPTER XXIV

Well, when I cleaned that rabbit for the fire, my bones was fair aching in me with a yearning that the boys might of been on deck to see that shot. Because everything was perfect. That doggone rabbit was about as far away as a revolver shot would carry, and I'd fired from the hip so easy and nacheral and careless as though I was never in want of any target easier than this here one. But no, there couldn't be anybody around except this old withered goat that had no good words for nobody and that would as soon cut his wrinkled throat as to pass a compliment along. He sat down and watched me roasting the rabbit.

"You ought to let the fire burn down and toast that flesh on wooden spits over the coals," says this old goat. "I never saw a grown up man that called himself a mountaineer, and that cooked meat like that!"

That was the way that he carried on—maddening. I had to keep one idea humming through my mind all of the time, which was that I was going to get this ranch into my own hands, one of these days, and that this was just one of the bits of nasty work that I had to accept for getting it. One more price to pay, and not the smallest price, either, you can bet!

But when I handed old Randal a stick with little chunks of roasted rabbit all along it, he takes one bite and then he says: "Why, this is a damned old buck of a rabbit that's been gallivanting around these hills for the last fifty years. I'd as soon try to eat leather! Gimme some of that bacon!" He ate bacon, then, with a lot of relish, and he left me to the rabbit. And it was the sweetest and the easiest rabbit eating that I pretty near ever done!

After that, we started on again in our rounds, and old Randal, he noticed everything: the condition of the fences, the amount of new fencing that had been done lately, the number of the cattle, and the amount of the fat that was on their ribs. Nothing missed him—nothing. He even seen the places along the edge of the water where some of them mired cows had been dragged out by the boys, and he seemed to be able to tell by the look of the spot just what had happened.

I was glad, you can bet, that I had had the boys working like beavers, lately. They had done half a year's work in that spell, and things looked pretty ship-shape.

Suddenly old Randal snarls at me, along towards evening when we was headed back for the ranch again: "Young feller, how long have you been with Harry?"

I told him, and he whistled.

"You been pretty busy, ain't you?"

"Busy?" says I. "Oh, no. You take a place like this, where all the boys are happy and contented, and where everything always runs along nice and oiled, things are kept up so well that it ain't much work."

He give me a grin, and his eyes wrinkled. "Son," says he, "I seen the looks of the cavvyard!"

No doubt those hosses *were* a little slab-sided and rough-coated from the work that I had given them. I had not thought of that, but you could trust this old chap to think of everything.

"These fellows are a free-riding lot," says I. "They wear out their spurs digging them through hoss-hide all the day long. And they work themselves and their hosses so careless that at the end of the day, when you might think that they had done enough riding and working, nothing will do them, but they have to get up races with each other. That's what wears down the hosses such a terrible lot. Hard on the hoss-flesh, but it keeps the boys feeling right, so I let 'em alone. You know how it is."

He only smiled. You wouldn't catch him making any damaging admissions.

"I'll tell you, Smith—or is your name Jones?"

Now, he had been switching from one name to another all day long: calling me Jones, and apologizing for not calling me Smith; calling me Smith and apologizing for not calling me Jones; that I'd got my own name sort of mixed up in my head, and I forgot what Harry Randal *had* called me—Smith or Jones.

"Sure," says I. "Jones is my name."

"I have a big place over yonder," said Henry Randal, "and I've tried out one manager after another. Now, sir, I tell you that place of mine is a man-sized job, but it hasn't some of the problems that *this* place has. It hasn't any mountains, like those yonder with the cañons, y'understand?"

I looked sidewise at him, and then nodded.

"Now, for a good up-and-coming man to work that place, I would pay a mighty handsome salary. I wouldn't start down low with an offer to a man like you, Smith—excuse me, I mean Jones. But right off, I'll offer you a hundred a month, and all found. That includes a little house all for your own, in case that you might happen to be the marrying kind of a man!"

That was all very nice and sweet, y'understand, but I just laughed at him. Me that was playing for the whole ranch in Sour Creek Valley, how was I to be contented with the prospect of being a hired man all of my life?

"More than that, eh?" says old man Randal. "Well, sir, I know that you've taken this place in hand and prevented my grandson from ruining it—"

"You know nothing of the kind," I put in.

He held up his hand.

"And I'll increase that offer of mine. I'll go right up to my top figure. I'll offer you four thousand a year, with everything in the way of a living expense thrown in free—horse, house, and a couple of servants. You hear me, young fellow?"

Now, if you know anything about conditions on the range, an offer like that was almost too good to be true. Back in the times when a cowpuncher got his forty-dollars a month, if he was lucky enough to have a job, the foreman of a great big outfit might get fifty or sixty, plus his house and his vegetable garden, and a couple of cows, if he was a married man. When a man got his promotion, it wasn't his increased pay that counted: it was the increased importance of the responsibilities that was dumped on his shoulders.

When you take all of these things into consideration, you can see how it was that when old Randal said to me that he would pay me as much as four thousand dollars a year!

It staggered me! And I thought it over very serious, because no matter for how much I could make out of the ranch, there was a big chance that I might not be able to make nothing at all if the rustlers got too thick for me, while four thousand a year was like a million, compared to what I had ever made before. But there was two things against it. One was that I would have to be working for this old crab; the other was that the gambling chance would be taken away from me—and what's life for a young man without the gambling chance?

Besides, he made me mad. It was only that he wanted to take me away from his grandson, and not because he had any idea that I could ever be worth any three or four thousand dollars a year to him.

I turned on Henry Randal and I says: "I have held in for a long time, and I can't hold in no more. I've heard you yapping and snarling and biting at my heels all day long, and now you want to take me away from Harry to work on your place. Now lemme tell you something: You offer me forty thousand dollars a year instead of four thousand, and I'll still tell you to be damned—and you may go to hell, Mr. Randal, sidewise, endwise, or any way that you please!"

"Good!" said Randal. "Of course I knew that Harry had been paying high for you, but I didn't guess *how* high."

"Ah," says I, with the light busting loose in my head all at once, "I suppose that I'm just a hired gun-fighter, eh?"

"You?" says Henry Randal, still blinking his bright bird-eyes at me, and still not seeming to be a bit mad at me for telling him what I thought. "Oh, no, you ain't a gun-fighter! D'you think that I could call a nice polite young gent like you by a wicked name? Not me, sonny, not me! You ain't a gun-fighter. You're a little woolly lamb, you are! No, Mr. Smith-Jones, or Jones-Smith, or whoever you are—I don't need to talk to you any more. I see that Harry has bought you, and a damned high price he must of paid. Only, young fellow, you want to be sure to collect your pay while your boss has the ready cash on hand!" And he began to cackle and nod to himself.

He was a wicked-looking old chap, right enough. Smart, too, but like most smart folks, he was apt to overreach himself. Because here he was writing me down as a bad fighting man, when as a matter of fact I was no hand with a gun at all. I've let you in on the ground floor and showed you the facts, and the only thing that was against me, ever, was some killings that wasn't really any fault of mine. They was sort of shoved onto me at close quarters. Besides, they didn't amount to much. However, old Randal had made up his mind, and during the rest of the ride, now and then he would bust out chuckling, very pleased with himself, the old rip.

When he got home to the ranch-house, we met Harry, and his face showed the strain that he had been under. He give me one wild look, and I shrugged my shoulders. I could answer for a good many things, but I couldn't answer for how many cows that old chap had been able to count. When we got inside, though, old Randal turned right loose. He didn't want his grandson to have any peaceful moments if he could help it.

"It looks to me, Harry," says he, "that you're at least fifty cows short. I won't be sure till I look over the herd to-morrow, so I want a good fast hoss ready at daybreak. But I should say that you are down about fifty—about fifty in the hole, my boy. And where are you going to get them in before to-morrow night, Harry? Where are you going to get them in?" And he began to rub his hands together and laugh, very pleased with himself.

Harry was white, he was so broke up and so scared. I went on up the stairs, because I didn't want to be in on any more of that family fight. I got to my room, and there was Pepillo with his fingers working like lightning and making a braid of horsehair for a chain. It was a relief to see him.

I went over to the window and leaned out to take a breath of air and cool off, for that old man had heated me up a lot, I can tell you! Then I heard old Randal talking at the window of the living-room just underneath me. I suppose that he had no idea my room was right over it.

He says: "You know all about this Smith, do you?"

"I know enough about him," says Harry, very gloomy.

"And you're glad to have him here?"

"Why not?" says poor Harry.

"Well, my son," says old Randal, "let me tell you that I know a bit more about range men than you ever could know, because you ain't born with the sense to know them and their ways. I tell you that this fellow is a bad one. A real bad actor, my boy. You've got him here working for a big price, but I tell you that before he's through with you, he'll collect a bigger price than you can afford to pay."

"What's he been saying?" asked Harry.

"He said something to a running rabbit that was more than a hundred yards away. He said it with a plain Colt, old son. And though that gun only spoke one word, the rabbit was ready to hear no more. You understand me?"

"He hit a rabbit on the wing with a Colt—more than a hundred yards off?" gasped Harry.

"He did," says old Randal pretty solemn. "Now, Harry, I know that you're about two-thirds rascal. But I don't care about that. If you got brains enough to run this ranch, I don't care what help you use. Only, I want to tell you that a chap who can shoot like that ain't honest. He's spent too much of his life practicing with guns—too much. He's a dangerous poison, my lad—and look out that you don't find it out for yourself!"

CHAPTER XXV

When I stood back from the window, there was Pepillo beside me, and he grinned at me.

"But did you really do it, señor?" says he.

"To the rabbit?" says I. "Yes—by luck. Nothing but a ten thousand to one shot that happened to land—and that's the truth. But between you and me, Pepillo, this here happy home of ours is about played out, and it's time for you and me to be thinking about travels."

"Why?" says Pepillo.

"Old Randal is a hawk," I told the kid. "Nothing misses his eyes. And he's seen enough to-day to know about how many cattle there are in the valley. Whatever else we can do, we can't get back the missing cattle, kid; and that means the end of Harry Randal's pipe-dream; and that means the end of you and me here. Where should we head for next?"

"Why, Big Boy," says Pepillo, "that would be giving up your hopes of the ranch, wouldn't it?"

I nodded.

"And that would break your heart," says Pepillo. "Would it not?"

"The stuff that my heart is made of," I says to him, "is not broken any too quick. It has been banged and hammered and stretched a good many times, but it's never broke yet and it's never going to break. You understand me, Pepillo?"

He nodded. "But," says the kid, "you can't tell. You may work something out to-night—some way of beating the game, and fooling Henry Randal. Why not keep hoping?"

Why not keep on hoping? Well, there was no good reason why that I shouldn't. It was easy to daydream. I hitched my heels onto the table in the center of the room, and I started blowing rings of smoke at the ceiling.

Says Pepillo: "There is a very fine sunset, señor."

"Damn the sunset," says I.

"All right," says Pepillo. "Now, if you were to have everything that you are dreaming about, what would it be?"

"You know, Pepillo. I would cultivate this here ranch like a garden. I would have it filled with the finest cows that ever walked!"

"That is something," says Pepillo. "But after all, cows cannot fill the heart of a man, can they?"

"I would fence in some of the flats down by the river," says I, "and I'd plant that rich ground there with orchard trees, and such stuff. I'd have three or four hundred acres under irrigation, Pepillo, and d'you know what that means?"

"It does not seem much," says Pepillo.

"Not much!" says I. "Well, kid, it would bring in about how many thousand of dollars a year?"

"How should I tell?" says Pepillo. "How should I know about such things—and why should I give a damn?"

And he makes a face at me. The pillow on the bed was handy and I chucked it at his head, but it missed, of course. You needed a bullet to tag that kid, he was so fast.

"It would bring in about twenty thousand dollars a year—that land alone!" says I to Pepillo.

"When you had all of that money, what would you do with it: the money from the cattle, and the money from the irrigated land, and all the rest. What would you do with it?"

"Why, son," says I, "I'd buy more land, for one thing. I'd buy up land on all sides, and I'd show the folks how to work a real big ranch in a real big way!"

"Very good," says Pepillo, "but if you had a million acres and a million dollars a year, then what would you do with the money?"

Now, I had never thought that far ahead, you see. I scratched my head and I thought it over, for a while.

I says: "Look here, Pepillo, I'd buy me some fancy togs, I can tell you."

"Clothes?" sneers Pepillo. "You could not spend very much money on them!"

"I would begin to breed fine fast hosses—and I would run them on the tracks."

"You have a million a year," says Pepillo. "You are spending only a little part of it!"

Well, that was true. Come to think of it, it would be pretty hard to spend that much money. I never had dreamed that far along the way.

"I would buy me a fine big house," says I.

"Isn't this house good enough?" says Pepillo.

"I would build one all of stone," says I.

"B-r-r!" says Pepillo. "It would be frightfully cold!"

"I would have furnaces in it."

"Stone houses are like prisons! If that house was so big, what would you have in it?"

"I would have some classy chromos hanging on the walls, and I would have rugs with a nap on 'em fetlock deep!"

"The better to catch all the dust in the world! And who would there be except the cowpunchers to enjoy the house with you?"

"I would get me a woman," says I.

"Bah!" says Pepillo. "You never could!"

"Look here, you little rat," says I to him, "you mean to say that no girl would have me?"

"No one able to appreciate oil paintings," says Pepillo. "No one—except a woman no better than one of your cowpunchers—you know! Unless you went out and *bought* a woman of education. Would you do that?"

"Why not?" says I.

"Faugh!" says Pepillo. "Would you have a bought woman around you?"

"Why not?" says I. "I've had a notice around the world, and I've seen that these here marriages that start with a heap of love, and the ones that start in with just a sort of business agreement, they turn out much different. Mostly all of them changes."

"That is a great lie, and the father, and the grandfather of all great lies," says Pepillo.

"Is it, kid?" says I. "Now you write this down. When a gent and a girl marries because they're in love, it means that they're just blind: and as soon as they begin to see the facts about each other, they are sick of each other, you can bet on that! And then the plate-throwing and the staying out at nights begins. No, kid, if I wanted a swell-looking girl to hold down this here house, I'd as soon go right out where they keep the market stocked up with that sort of female—"

"Bah!" snorts Pepillo. "You talk like they were cattle!"

"Maybe I do," says I. "I got a lot of respect for a good cow! Anyway, I would go right out and I would mix up with some of the fancy families. I would say: "Here I am with a million a year; healthy, sound, fairly good-natured, but set on having my own way. I want a wife—want one that knows how to run a house, buy swell clothes and jewels, talk fancy about Dago music, and tell you why an oil painting beats a colored photograph all hollow. Have you got anything for me to look at? My banker is Blank and Blank!' Now, kid, when I got through with that spiel, just one thing would stick in the heads of a lot of them—they would think only about that million dollars. They would fetch out their best girls. 'A million dollars!' they would say in the ear of the girl. And then when she looked at me, she wouldn't see that I was bow-legged and rolled my own. All she would see would be flowers and a million a year; and I would have my pick. I would simply look her over."

"It is horrible," says Pepillo, narrowing his eyes at me. "But what sort of a woman would you pick out, eh?"

"Something pretty," says I, "but not too damn good looking, because I don't want all the fancy gents on the range getting lovesick and such stuff. Nope, I want a good, healthy, bright girl, not too full of dreams, fond of children, sound feet and hands, good teeth. Somebody that sleeps well at night, don't groan when you get up early, and meets you with a smile when you come in at night, and makes a fuss over you like the house hadn't got on very good while you was away!"

I stopped and got rid of a big yawn.

"Is that all that you want?" says Pepillo. "She will run away with another man inside of six months."

"You're crazy," says I. "After she's gone through the motions of being in love with me for six months, she *will* be in love. You take a girl, and you start in with a dream and she winds up wide awake. But you start in by telling a girl all the facts about what she is gunna expect, and she begins with being wide awake, and she is apt to wind up in a dream. At least, the chances are pretty good that way, and I'd take the chance, if I had the money. I see that you don't approve?"

"That," said Pepillo slowly, "is the talk of a pig—not of a man!"

"All right, son," says I. "When you get a mite older, you'll find out that men are a whole lot nearer to pigs than they are to angels—and you can take it straight from me. Angels is things that I never could understand *at* all, but pigs, they is something that I could always sympathize with."

"I see," says Pepillo, nodding to himself. "The point is that you have never *seen* a real woman!"

"Me? Dozens of 'em, kid, and held 'em in my arms; and told 'em that I couldn't live without 'em; and stayed awake all night aching at heart for them. I've left 'em feeling that I would die if I didn't see 'em in twenty-four hours. But I never died, kid—I lived and got fat, instead. And this love stuff is just so much bunk."

"Bah!" says Pepillo. "I have heard fools talk like that before. But if you were to see a real woman—one such as I mean—I think that you would change your mind, eh?"

CHAPTER XXVI

Speaking of women, the way that we had been doing, just then, it was sort of queer, the interruption that we had. A ruction busted out not far away, and when I got out to the hall, I seen Harry Randal trying to pacify his grandfather, but the old man was wild.

"By God," says he, "it's a crime and a shame, and you planned it out to spoil my stay at your house—and you wanted to drive me away the quicker by putting me into this room. Damnation, I never heard of such a low trick. Look where I've been put!"

He goes back into the room, still jabbering, and I went along with him and Harry.

"It was the room of Stephen's wife!" yells Henry Randal. "And I never could abide her, and you know it; and she never could abide me. Ain't that her picture hanging there on the wall? But damn me if I ever suspected anything or so much as looked around me, until I happened to open that closet for curiosity—"

I looked at the picture on the wall. It was of a mighty pretty, dark-faced girl, very slim, and very good-looking in every way—smiling, and gay, y'understand? That picture was pretty faded and it was all dressed up in old-fashioned clothes, but even so it give my heart a thrill. I looks it over and then I turns around and stares at the closet which old Randal had throwed open. Scarlet, yellow, lavender, blue, crimson, white, brown, gold and a dozen other colors, that closet was pack full of all of the fine clothes of a woman, and old Randal, he was roaring: "There they are! Damn my heart, if I don't even *recognize* some of them! That there damned yaller lace thing was

151

what she was wearing the time that I told her what a woman's place was in a house, and she reminded me that this was not my house! Yes, sir, and that infernal white affair, it's what she was married in—and I wish that I had never seen that day. Didn't I have a foreboding? I said to Stephen on that day: 'Steve, I don't wish you any bad luck, but isn't she a mite too pretty to be good?' That was what I said, and Steve would never forgive me for saying it! Not to his death-day! And here you've put me jam up into this room—on purpose—to drive me away home. But I won't be driven! I'll stay—a month! Ay, and there's the damned perfume that she always wore filling the room and choking me!"

It was jasmine, a thin, light fragrance of it that you had to think twice about before you could realize what was the sweetness that was coming towards you.

I went back into the other room and I sat down and closed my eyes.

"You look sad," says Pepillo.

"Jasmine!" says I. "I've never smelled that stuff without seeing again all the pretty girls that I've ever been in love with, and without sorrowing after the whole lot of them."

"So!" says Pepillo, "and yet you would say that you are not a great calf!"

The ruction about the wrong room was straightened out, after a while, and the old mean devil was lodged in another room, with Harry sweating blood before the job was finished. He come back to my room and stood in the door for a minute.

"Well, Big Boy," he says, "are you thinking?"

"I'm thinking," says I.

"For God's sake, do something," says he. "Because thinking would never make up the difference. He's got my bank statement!"

"And he'll be able to count the cows, and that will straighten things out for him. He'll know that you're failing."

"He will."

"Harry," says I, "there's such a thing as money in banks!"

"Sure," says he. "If you know how to sign the right checks to get at it!"

"Yes," says I, "or how to hold a gun at the right head."

"Shut up—the kid!" says he.

"Pepillo won't talk no more than you nor me. He's sworn to me, and I'd trust him, old timer, farther than I would trust myself!"

Yes, sir, that was a fact, and it give me such a warm feeling to know that the kid would stick by me as much as me by him, that I reached out to lay a hand on his shoulder. But he glided away from beneath my touch. He was always like that. Reaching for him was like reaching for a shadow. However, he turned and smiled a little at me, but his eyes was big and his lips was pinched with excitement.

"You mean—" says Harry, trembling on the edge of what he hoped but what he didn't dare to say.

"I mean that I'll have enough money here to make up for the difference between the stock that you have and the stock that you had ought to have. And I'll get it by stealing if there's no other way," says I. "Let's see first what he is able to count on the range. See how short he writes us down. And when he has finished, you tell him that you've made a sale of more than the missing number, and the next day you'll show him the cash for them. You understand? And then I'll dig up the cash that night—"

Harry came up to me and held out his hand. His voice fair trembled.

"God, Big Boy," says he, "what a man you are!"

I couldn't shake hands with him. I just despised and hated him too much. So I pretended not to see his hand, and I rolled a cigarette until he left the room.

Pepillo ran up to the door the minute that it closed, and he done a war dance there, and stuck out his tongue at the thought of Harry Randal, and pretended to drive a knife through the heart of that thought, and then to cut its throat. Very vicious and concentrated with meanness.

When he finished, he turned around and he says:

"A pig! Ah, what a pig, señor!"

"You was calling me a pig, a while ago," says I.

"No," says Pepillo. "You are only—how shall I say it? —what word is big enough for it? You are only the greatest dam-fool that ever lived in this world. That is all that you are!"

Nice talk, that, from a kid like him to his boss and friend. But I didn't mind what Pepillo said, somehow. He might be right, and I might know his rightness. But just the same, it didn't rile me so much to hear the truth from him.

I slept pretty good, that night, and when I got downstairs in the morning, we found out that the old man had left the house. He was gone, and he would be making his round. He had made part of it the day before. And by the middle of the afternoon, he was back with that mean look of his wrote all over his face.

"It seems to me, Harry," says he, "that allowing for a decent amount of care, you should have at least fifty-eight more cows than you have at the present time. I wonder if you're too busy to explain that little mystery to me?"

That was the way he talked—smooth, and careless, and calm, but with an icy devil in his voice and in his eye, which was saying to Harry, every minute, "You've lost your game and you've lost your bet—and you're no good!"

"You can't make up your mind on hearsay like that!" says Harry, sweating all over. "You've got to give me a chance to make a clear accounting, Grandfather! You've *got* to give me a chance!"

"Sure," says the old devil. "I'll give you all the chance that you want. You can start your roundup right now this afternoon and clear the cows away towards the ranch. By noon tomorrow we can have an *exact* accounting."

And suddenly the tall old chap walks up to Harry and lays a hand on his shoulder.

"Harry, Harry," says he, in a voice that shakes a little and comes from deeper than his toes, "do you think that I *want* you to lose? No, lad, but I want you to prove to me that you *are* a man, and that I'm not the last one of the true Randal blood left on the face of this unhappy earth!"

I disremember when anything ever jarred me so much as that little speech done, or took me so by surprise, since one time I started to brush a square-built Dutchman out of my way, down in a crowd at a rodeo, and he turned around and slammed me with a perfect right hook that hung itself on the edge of my chin, and turned out the lights for half a minute. But this was even more of a surprise. I had begun to figger that this here old chap was one of the kind that ain't got anything human about them.

And here he was, turning up with something deep, and something decent, too.

When I come out of my trance, the boys was climbing into their saddles, to start on the round-up. And I begun to ride out along with them, pretty thoughtful. When it came to cheating Henry Randal the way that I had been planning with Harry on doing—well, it was one thing to hand a package to a cold-blooded fish like I thought that he was, and it was another thing to fool with a man that really had some sort of a feeling for the folks of his own kin. It give me a flash of that old codger who might be as hard as flint in most ways, but down deep in his heart he was sort of yearning and praying to find out if Harry Randal might not be worthy of being his heir. And what sort of a hound would I be if I was to help at a low-down trick, like this?

I was thinking these things over, when I see a commotion among several of the boys that was ahead of me, and then I see that Joe Maxwell, a puncher that had been out riding range that afternoon, had just rode up to them and he was saying something that excited them a good deal.

Then they all turned around and come spilling for me as fast as they could quirt their broncos along. They come rushing around me, and the first one to me is Shorty, yelling: "Hey, Big Boy, there's a flock of cows come down from the hills into this here damn valley—" That was enough to make even Shorty forget how he had been hating me, lately. Then here was Joe Maxwell, saying the same story all over again.

What he had to say read like a fairy story. He said that in the upper valley he had come across a herd of an even hundred cows that wore the Sour Creek brand, and of calves that didn't have no brand at all on them.

"There's only one way to figure it out," says Maxwell. "These cows and calves are part of the herds that the rustlers have got away from us and from other gents in the ranches near by us, and these have got loose and have wandered down into their own old range, and here they are!"

I couldn't believe it. Not till I had tin-canned along with the rest of the bunch and come into sight of that same bunch.

There wasn't any doubt about it, then. There was a bunch of maybe fifteen Sour Creek cows, wearing their brands all proper. And the rest was calves up to yearlings. They was going along pretty slab-sided, as if they'd been in some sort of a place where the forage wasn't any too fat. They was going along with their heads down, mowing that grass clean, in front of them, and making every lick count, now that they was down here in good grass, again.

Anyway, after one good long look at them, I decided that this part of the mystery would have to take care of itself, because the one thing that really mattered was that these here cows and calves would more than make up for the lacking numbers in the herd of Harry Randal —and with that deficit covered, Harry was O.K., and so was I!

I wrote that thought down in red in my mind, and then I told the boys to hurry along with the round-up, while I went to hunt up Harry, and to tell him the good news.

CHAPTER XXVII

What that news done was to wipe about ten years off of the face of Harry Randal. He begun to laugh like a child, and away he kited to take a look at the new herd.

"We'll ask no questions," says Harry Randal, "but if *I* was the foreman of this ranch, I would have my men oil up their guns, because it's a pretty safe bet that the folks that lost these cows and all of those calves is gunna come looking for them, and they'll come with their gats ready for action!"

I didn't have to be a college graduate to understand as much as this. I spread the word around among the boys, and they were certainly willing. Fighting was ice cream and cake to that tough gang, and they were living every day in expectancy of something big in the way of bullets flying.

In the meantime, that round-up went along in swinging style. We cleaned out the upper end of the valley pretty well, and it wasn't hard to do, because most of the cows, for some reason, had wandered down Sour Creek and they was already bunched pretty close to the ranch-house. I left out a few pickets to keep the main bunches from drifting south again during the night, and then we all turned in very tired, but very happy.

And even Pepillo, who never paid much attention to what was happening in the line of business on the ranch, he seemed pretty gay, and he would rock back his head and open up a song that shortened the miles, coming home. There was never anybody to sing much better than that kid. It just rose up and flowed out from him with no more trouble than out of a singing bird. And it made you happy to listen. It was like closing your eyes on a rainy day and *feeling* sunshine right on your face.

It was a funny thing to watch old Henry Randal that night at the supper table. He knew that something was up. He could tell it by the high spirits in Harry, for one thing, and he would of given a lot to understand what that mystery was, but he couldn't bring himself to ask.

It wasn't long after supper that I turned in, and feeling the way that I did, tired but happy, with the feeling that the job was about done, and the ranch already mine for keeps, I was asleep about as quick as my head hit the pillow, there I lay dreaming about really having the million a year to spend that I had talked about with Pepillo.

What waked me up, finally, was the feeling of a strong draft across my face, and when I opened my eyes, there was a small light shining on my face. I sat up in bed, and there in the doorway I saw a dream with my eyes open!

Yes, what I mean to say is that I seen a thing that couldn't be real, and I knew it couldn't be real, but still, there it was right before me. It was a young girl, about eighteen, say, or nineteen—a dark-eyed, black-haired girl with more beauty in her face than I ever seen before, or than I ever dreamed of. She was dressed in a sort of a dress of yellow lace that left her shoulders and her arms all bare, and to the day I die, I'll never forget the look of her hand, that was cupped around the flame of the candle that she held. And I remember, too, how the highlights slipped and glimmered along her arms, and how her eyes glistened as the light struck up against them.

Well, the sight of her lifted me out of my bed like a strong hand and set me on my feet. She seemed to be peering into that room, hunting something, but she didn't seem to see it, and when her eyes fell on me, she looked right through me, as though I was nothing at all. She looked right through me, and then she turned around and she went down the hall towards the stairs.

I got to the door of my room in one long stride, and as I got to it, I had a breath of a mighty small, faint perfume, that I had breathed not very long before. It was jasmine, and right then I knew what had happened. The ghost of that girl—the dead wife of Stephen Randal—she had come back to haunt that house, and it wasn't no living hand that carried the candle down the stairs in front of me; and it wasn't no living light, either.

That was why the dress that she was wearing was so old-fashioned and that was why she moved without making no sound.

I sneaked to the head of the stairs, and at the bottom, she turned and she smiled up to me. It was as though the distance and the shadow didn't let her see that it was only the rough-neck and the cowpuncher, Blondy Kitchin. It was as though she thought I was somebody that she loved. Because there was real love in her face: it parted her lips and let me see the gleam of her teeth, and it flared up in her eyes, too; and she raised a hand and beckoned to me.

Once when I was a kid I come home pretty late at night, and I was scared to go inside. I stood out in the garden. It was autumn, and mighty cold with the first frost in the air, but the roses was still living that would be killed by that frost, and as I stood there, I was shivering with the cold and turning to ice inside and all the same, the breath of them roses out of the dark, it flowed into my blood and it made my heart ache with happiness and with sorrow.

That was the way that I felt when I stood up there at the head of the stairs and looked down to her. I felt like my heart was breaking because I was so scared and I was so sad; and yet I was never half so happy in my whole life. I felt that if I come close enough to her I would find that the fragrance of the jasmine, it wasn't sprinkled on the dress that she wore, but it was breathed into the air by the ghost itself!

There is a saying, you know, that if you follow a ghost that beckons, you'll be dead before the morning light ever finds you. I thought of that, too; but still, nothing could hold me when I seen her raise her arm.

I started down those stairs, and she turned away, without hurrying, and went towards the outside door.

The light of that candle was gone when I got to the downstairs, and I reached the front door in one jump. It seemed to me that the smell of the jasmine was there in front of me. I went outside, and still that perfume seemed to be hanging just before me, while I hurried up and down in the garden.

I dunno how long I was there—not very long, I sup-

pose. But anyway, finally I looked up and seen the cold
old moon watching me. That seemed to bring me to my
senses. I turned around and went back to my room. I
lighted the lamp, but somehow, I couldn't stand the rush
of that light. It seemed to kill the happiness that was in
me, and the pain, too; and I wanted to keep the pain and
the joy, both of them.

I would of busted with it, though. I had to have somebody to talk to, even if it was only a kid, so finally
I waked up Pepillo. He sat up and damned me.

"Pepillo," says I, "for God's sake, talk soft, or you'll
scare the thought of her away from me!"

"The thought of what?" says Pepillo, and yawns.

"The thought of a ghost, Pepillo," says I. "She come
to the door of this here room, and I seen her. It was the
dead wife of Stephen Randal, kid. Don't you talk back to
me. Don't you snicker or laugh, or I'll choke you. I swear
I will. Sit here," says I to the kid, "and gimme hold of
your hand to keep, will you?"

He done his cussing under his breath, but he sat down
there beside me. I told him all over again, and then again.

"You've felt this way before," says Pepillo, "and you've
got well of it again. You've fallen in love with girls and
out again, very *pronto,* and you'll fall out of love with
this fool ghost of yours, Big Boy."

I shook my head. "Words ain't of much account, old
son," says I, "but I tell you that this is different. Because
the others, they bothered me. I didn't want to lie awake
on account of them. But I tell you, I'd lie awake till I die,
if I could keep seeing the thought of this here ghost,
Pepillo. And so long as I live, kid, I'll never look at no
other woman."

Nothing mattered to that kid. He was so hard nails
would be soft compared to him; he was so hard he would
of laughed at a funeral going by; but even Pepillo seemed
to be sort of worked up by what I had to say. He caught
his breath.

"So, señor," says he, "when I grow to be a man, I shall
find one woman, and I shall love her as you love this
ghost. Hush, señor; you groan; and are you very sick?"

Sick? Ay, you might call it sickness. I didn't care
whether I lived or died.

"Oh, Blue Jay," says I, "how come that God could
ever of made anything so beautiful and so perfect as that

girl and then let her die? He couldn't let her die, and that's why she's got the power of coming back to earth, now and then! Pepillo, if I thought that praying would bring her back, for one second, I would pray, Pepillo!"

"Bah," says Pepillo. "Now you talk like a crazy man. Besides, you never knew a prayer. Confess that!"

"I confess it," says I. "Sit quiet, will you? I got to talk to you some more about her!"

He give my hand a pressure with his cold little fingers, and I says: "I waked up with a breath of wind in my face, and a ghost of a fragrance of jasmine, Pepillo—"

And God knows how long that I went on talking like that. Until finally, the first thing that I knew, something glittered against my eyes, and it was the rising sun, flashing from the pane of my window. I blinked around me, and there was Pepillo, with his hand still locked in mine, and smiling at me very gentle and kind.

I felt like a wonderful fool, but the kid didn't mock me. You could feel in Pepillo that no matter what a devil of a Blue Jay and a mischief-maker he was, when it come to anything important, he would understand.

The first thing I did was to sneak into that old room of dead Stephen Randal's dead wife. And there I looked at her picture on the wall. But I closed my eyes. I couldn't turn away quick enough. No, the camera had lied terrible about her, and there was more truth and beauty in the little finger of the ghost than in the picture on the wall.

I opened the door of the closet, and the jasmine breathed out around me. That was different. It seemed truer, and sadder. And while I stood there with my eyes closed, I could see her once more at the bottom of the stairs with her lips parting for love of me as she smiled up, and her hand raised.

Doggone me, it made me weak. I tell you true: I wanted to cry like a fool!

CHAPTER XXVIII

What did I know about love? I thought that I'd known everything, and I found out that I knew just nothing at all. I'd come up and knocked on the door a lot of times, but I'd never gotten inside of the house. Well, I was in, now, and the looks of everything was all different, I can tell you.

When I come down the stairs, I stood in a trance, looking out the window and listening to a doggone meadow lark that was singing outside the front of the house. I had heard meadow larks before, a lot of times, of course; but this here lark was made particular to sing for me. I says to Pepillo: "Did you ever hear a lark sing so mighty well as that, kid?"

The Blue Jay laughed. He never missed a chance for laughing, you understand. "You look sick," says he. "Is the singing as bad as all of that?"

We got outside, and there I was standing and looking at the blue of the morning sky, and at the shapes of the clouds; feeling, somehow, that they must be as lonely in the wind, up there, as I was lonely down below on the ground. How come that a growed up man should have thoughts like that? It was love, aching inside of me.

"Blue Jay," says I, "you done me a lot of good last night, but I still need some help for to-day. Stick close beside me!"

He done it, too, and he acted like I never seen him before, extreme kind and understanding.

"It's what you told me," says I to the Blue Jay. "I found a real woman. None of the rest ever counted. This is the first one, y'understand!"

"Ah, well," says Pepillo, "when I grow up, God help me to find a woman I can love as you love this one!"

"Time may wear the feeling away," says I.

"No," says Pepillo. "It will never die in you, I think."

And he said it so serious and so grave that I couldn't help more than half believing him.

I was glad that we had the round-up to take my thoughts away from myself, this day. We scoured up the valley and got the rest of the cattle into shape for counting. Well, old Henry Randal was out there himself, and he worked himself almost blind, trying to count fewer than he had seen the day before. But he couldn't do it, and he couldn't make out what was different, because we had sifted the new cows and calves very thorough through the rest of the herd, and he couldn't tell any difference. Except that where he had counted the cows about sixty below par the day before, he now had to admit that the numbers was about forty more than could of been expected.

Finally, he rode up to Harry Randal, and there was a happy light in his eye.

"Harry," says he, "I think that you're beating me, and I thank God for it! And maybe you're right about him—because if he can turn tricks like this, he may be just the sort of a poison that's needed here on Sour Creek!"

As for Harry Randal, he was almost turning himself inside out, he was so happy. But he had to take a chance to snarl at me.

"You get the credit from the old man for this," says he, "but you know and I know that it was just the damnedest piece of luck that ever come to any man. And if my luck is coming in, I'm gunna play it and play it hard!"

Oh, he was a fine chap, that Harry Randal. I says to him: "Your opinion is like the opinion of your grandfather, as far as I'm concerned. I don't give a damn what it is. I'm in Sour Creek to do a job, and I'm gunna do it, but I'll take no lip from you on the way, Randal!"

Oh, what a black look he give me! If he'd had the power, he would of liked to chaw me up fine, I can tell you! But, in the meantime, I was pretty busy. We had the cows now, but how long would we be able to keep them?

What I did right on the spot was to hire four kids from

Sour City—four boys along about fourteen to fifteen years old. It was vacation time—I got them for almost nothing —and I told them what I wanted them to do. They could be counted on to keep wider awake than any ordinary cowpuncher; they was so proud to be used to keep a watch against the rustlers that they pretty nearly busted.

I had each of the four posted on a high hill towards the head of the valley of Sour Creek, and they could look clean across to one another, and into the cañons, and down towards the ranch. I had each of the boys pile up two heaps of brush, close together. One brush was of dead twigs and brushes. That pile was covered with a tarpaulin and it was kept with a little can of oil near by. In the night, if the kid was to see or hear anything suspicious, he was to throw the oil on the pile of dried brush and to light it quick. The blaze of the fire would be seen at the ranch-house, where I kept a lookout, night and day, and relieved him every four hours, to make sure that he would be able to keep his eyes open. But if there was trouble in the day, the kids were to light the dry brush and then heap on from the second pile, which was all green stuff, and which would raise a column of smoke big enough to be seen fifty miles away!

Well, that wasn't all. Each of them had a double-barreled shotgun, and he was ordered to have it with him, night and day. In case that he was surprised, so that he didn't have a chance to light the heap, he was to fire off that gun—one barrel if he could, or two barrels. Then the other kids would be sure to hear the noise, and *they* would light their fires and send their signal down the valley to the ranch-house.

Every day, Shorty, or Rusty McArdle, or me, we rode the rounds and inspected those kids, and they liked it a lot. We brought them plenty of chuck and ammunition, so's they could practice "killing rustlers" all day long. And then we looked over their shotguns and praised the way they kept them, and admired how neat and soldier like they done everything—and those four kids was so proud that you couldn't hardly touch them.

They seemed to be doing the work, too, because for five days things kept up like this and there was no sign of a rustler running cows out of the valley. Not no sign at all!

Harry Randal begun to breathe easier. He couldn't

kick at the sum of money that I was giving as wages to the boys, and he had to admit that it was a fine scheme. So, during those five days, things got so that I didn't have much to worry about, except Shorty, and the mean way that he had with me, but I was almost glad to have Shorty acting sour, like this, because anything that helped to take my mind away from the ghost of Stephen Randal's wife was pretty welcome to me.

However, I pretty near had a show-down with Shorty the day after the round-up. How it come was that me and Shorty spotted a fool steer that had bogged down and we worked on him together till we got him onto firm footing, and then the idiot lit out and chased us as if we was his mortal enemies. We managed to dodge away from him, though, and we sat our hosses on a hump of ground and laughed at that doggone idiot as he went tearing across the plain, throwin' his head and acting like he had just conquered the world, instead of only being pulled out of a mud hole!

Well, the laugh sobered right out of the face of Shorty, when he woke up to the fact that he was out here alone with me. He give me his worst black look.

And then he starts to ride away.

"Hey, Shorty!" says I. "Come back here!"

He turns around in the saddle and glowers at me.

"I can hear you from over here," says he. "What you want?"

"Look here," says I, "tell me what I've done to Pepillo that's made you so damned hot against me?"

I thought that he would bust. He was so mad that he turned red and then he turned white.

"Ain't you got no shame?" says Shorty. "I know that you got no decency nor cleanness, but my God, I would think that in a man of your size there might be a little room for shame, you know!"

That was enough to make most folks fight, but I wasn't in fighting mood.

I says: "Now, Shorty, I wouldn't take that much from most folks, but I'll tell you straight that I like the way that you stick up for Pepillo, though I'm damned if I know why you've buried the hatchet against him!"

"You don't know?" snarls Shorty. "You don't know? Like hell you don't! And why do you keep up the bluff, talking to me like this here?"

"What bluff?" says I.

"What bluff?" screamed Shorty.

He wrung his hands together and finally he was able to get his madness down under control so that he could speak again. And he says to me: "Now, Big Boy, I want you to know that the only reason that I don't try to put a slug of lead through you, the way that I had ought to do, is the kid won't let me. I've begged for a chance at you, but the only answer is No. Now, if there's ever a change of mind, and I get permission, the first thing that I do will be to tap at your door and tell you to come out with your shooting irons."

"Shorty," says I, "you're crazy!"

"Because you're one of these here dead shots?" says Shorty. "Oh, I know that stuff, and how you killed the rabbit a hundred yards away. But that ain't what counts with me. I can't kill a rabbit at a hundred yards, but I can kill a man at twenty, and I'm gunna come trying when I get the word."

I should of argued with him, but I couldn't. I was getting too mad myself. "Well, you come along whenever you're ready," says I.

"And I got this to say," says Shorty, as he turns his hoss away, "I've mixed with some low-down skunks, but you're the lowest. You're so low that you could stand up straight and walk right under the belly of a snake and never touch the top of your hat!"

That's what Shorty said to me on this day. And I went back to the ranch in a daze. Who was the kid? Who was he that he could make Shorty go wild, like this? A younger brother? No! A young nobleman? No, that seemed wrong, too. God knew what the answer to the riddle was.

And I couldn't tell that I was mighty close to having everything explained, and explained in a way that would clear it all from start to finish: clear it in a single word; make it all easy to see. Only—right at that minute I was a million miles away from knowing what the single word could be. Just as you're a million miles from knowing that word, too.

CHAPTER XXIX

For five days, then, everything had gone pretty well, and I was set for smiling at the whole world, with the exception of the trouble with Shorty, and I hoped that in time I should be able to see a way to smooth even that over, pretty well. I really began to think that I had beaten the game—God forgive me, because right then was when the blow fell.

I mustn't get ahead of the game. When I come to write about the terrible time that was coming, I want to go slow and easy, and show you everything just as it happened, beginning with the night that I waked up and found Pepillo sneaking out of the room.

He always slept yonder in a corner of the room, sticking to his goatskins, though I noticed that finally he sneaked a mattress under the skin, and so he was fixed pretty comfortable.

I should never of noticed him moving this night, because when the Blue Jay decided on moving without noise, he was more silent than a flying owl; but ever since the ghost had looked in on me, there hadn't been a single night that I slept really sound, because all of the time I was sort of expecting that she might appear before me again, and that if I was too sound asleep I would miss her.

Anyway, my eyes opened before I had heard a thing, and I seen the shadow of Pepillo stand up.

He come over to my bed and leaned there a minute, and then he shoved a little piece of paper under my pillow. After that, he went for the door, stepping mighty silent. He didn't seem to be expecting anything behind him, though, because when I rose up from my bed, he jumped sideways almost to the wall and whirled around on me with a gasp.

I just shut the door and locked it and dropped the key into my pocket.

"All right, kid," says I, "where was you going?"

"No place," says Pepillo, like a fool boy.

I lighted the lamp, and while I was doing it, he made a step for my bed and snatched beneath the pillow. He missed, though. And then I picked up the pillow and I found the paper that had been put there. It threw Pepillo into a good deal of excitement.

"It is only a joke, señor!" says he. "It means only nothing."

"That's why you're shaking so bad, then?" says I, looking him over. Because he was extreme white and unsteady. He was dressed for a trip, too, belt and all, though his clothes was put on not so sassy as usual. I opened the paper and I read:

"Big Boy, I'm sorry to sneak off in the night, but it saves a lot of arguing and explaining. You and I have got along pretty fine. I'm sorry that I can't tell you all about everything, and now I know that I'll never be able to explain to you. Well, best of luck to you, old timer. You're going to beat the game here and make yourself rich. Then you build your house and get your pictures and buy your horses and your woman. So long. Pepillo."

"Short *and* snappy," says I to the kid.

"I'm sorry," says the Blue Jay.

"Well, what's wrong?" says I.

He shrugged his shoulders.

"What have I done to hurt your feelings this time?" says I, "because if you'll explain, I'll apologize. I got no pride, where you're concerned, Blue Jay."

Well, the Blue Jay leaned against the wall and he hid his eyes behind his hand.

"Look here," says I, "you're homesick. Is that it? You got an idea that you have to go to see your own people. Now, I'd be right tickled to pay your way out to see them, wherever they may be, and back again. If you'll come back!"

"I need no money," says Pepillo. "Only—I shall be glad to go."

"You'll come back, then?" says I.

"Ah, yes," says Pepillo.

"Look me in the eye," says I, "and then say that over again. Slow and steady!"

"I shall—come—back!" says Pepillo. But he couldn't work the bluff. He broke down. His strength, it faded out of him, and it left him pretty weak.

"Look me in the eye!"

He couldn't do it at all.

"You damn little liar," says I. "You *wouldn't* come back."

"Señor! Señor!" says the Blue Jay, getting terrible excited, but fighting to keep from showing it. "I must go."

"You must *not* go," said I.

I thought he would drop, he seemed so scared.

"You must not go," says I. "You think that you have to, but down in your heart you know that you don't want to go!"

"Ha!" says Pepillo. "Why do I not want to go?"

"Because you're happy here."

"And what, pray, should make me happy here?"

"Because you got room for your nacheral meanness to bust loose, out here on the range."

"I am to be happy here? *I* am to be happy here? I tell you, señor, that this is a dull and a stupid life to me. I'm tired of it, and I desire to go."

"Are you tired of me, too, Blue Jay?"

"Why should I not be? Yes, I am tired of you, too. Will you unlock the door, señor?"

It cut me pretty deep and quick, of course. I got up and I shoved the key into the lock, but I pulled it out again.

"No," said I.

"Pah!" said Pepillo, "what shall I do to prove that I do not wish to stay?"

"Come here," says I.

He come swaggering across the room and he stood there in front of me with his head chucked back and his legs braced far apart, and a sort of a sneer on his lips. There was never nobody that could look more like a sassy devil than that Pepillo, as maybe I've said before.

"I am here, señor."

"Now, then, you been happy here, before?"

"Yes, for a time."

"What's changed you, then?"

He looked me right in the eye.

"Do you think that I can live forever listening to the cursing and the stupid talk of cowpunchers? No, they are very stupid and tiresome. I have had enough of it."

"And of me, too, Pepillo?"

"Why not?" says the kid. "Are you very different from the rest of them?"

"I don't believe you, Blue Jay," says I. "I think that you're lying to me. You don't really mean that you're tired of me."

He flew into a rage.

"Bah!" says he. "I have never heard of such a pig of a man! Could I not be tired of you? And do you think I have ever forgotten that you dared to strike me—me?"

He snapped his fingers under my nose.

It made me terrible mad. I jumped up and grabbed him by the wrist. "I got half a mind to flog you again, damn your sassy hide!" says I. "There's the key. Unlock the door and get the hell out of here and never come back again."

"Good!" says he.

He jammed the key into the lock, but he couldn't quite find the place, and I heard the key chatter once or twice against the lock. I grabbed him by the shoulder and spun him around. Yes, sir, there was tears in his eyes! So I knocked that key out of his hand and put my foot on it.

"Pepillo," says I, "you're the grandest nacheral born liar in this here world!"

I couldn't tell you how the Blue Jay looked at me, with his lips trembling, and his eyes softening, but with a sort of a despair in his face.

"No, no, Big Boy. I do not want to go, but I *must* go."

"You must go—and never come back? Now how come that that is possible? Look here, kid," says I, "I dunno how it is, but there ain't much that I wouldn't give up for you. Y'understand? Now, if you was to tell me how I could make things so that—"

He shook his head.

"There is nothing that even you can do," says he. "Only, I must go."

"You must *not* go—and I tell you, Pepillo, that I won't *let* you go."

It seemed to throw a tremendous scare into him.

"B-b-big Boy," stammered Pepillo. "Will you believe me? Will you please believe me, in the name of God, when I swear to you that if I do not go to-night, you will die before morning? Oh, I swear that that is true! So let me go! Let me go!"

I *did* believe that there might be something in what the Blue Jay said. There was a sort of a mystery all wrapped around him, like he wouldn't bring no good luck to nobody. And then besides, there was a ghostly feeling in me ever since the image of the dead woman trailed the perfume of jasmine into the room and down the stairs into the night.

"All right, Blue Jay," says I, "then I'll die, since it's my turn to take chances again."

He shook his head. He was fair dancing up and down, in his impatience.

"They are waiting for me now!" gasped Pepillo. "I must go. I am already late, late, late! Ah, no, señor. I was only a fool to tell you this. I should have known that I could not frighten you. Only I tell you not—for pity of yourself and for me, let me go!"

"Will you explain to me," says I, "how it could be a mercy to you to let you go? Is your life threatened, too?"

"Ay," says the Blue Jay, "because I should never be happy so long as I lived!"

I stepped back and stared at him. No, there wasn't any doubt about him being sincere, now. It was wrote all over his face, that he meant exactly what he had said.

I tried to understand. "Blue Jay," says I, "I think that you're serious, but I can't make up my mind about it. I swear to God that I want only to do what's right by you—but you've lied so often to me—"

"I'm telling you only the very truth, now," says Pepillo. "I shall swear by the cross—"

Into that last speech of his there cut a sharp sound of a whistle from the night beyond the house, and it was just as though a whip had slashed across the Blue Jay.

"They have come!" says Pepillo. "Now—now—let me go."

He was fair shaking. He wanted to get out into the dark, and still he was afraid to go.

"Tell me who *they* are," says I, "and I may let you go."

"I can only tell you," says the Blue Jay, "that they are men who will wait not ten seconds, and then they will kill us both, señor."

Half I felt that he must be right, and yet I was afraid

to let him go. Somehow, down in my boots, I felt that he was trying to sacrifice himself, in some way, for my safety, and I couldn't stand for him doing that, of course. I put my back against the door and shook my head.

"The door is locked, Blue Jay," says I. "And here we stay, if it's going to come to a pinch like this. Let them get you if they can!"

CHAPTER XXX

Of course I meant what I said, and then I stepped to the window and shouted: "Hey, boys! Shorty! Rusty!"

Because my voice was sure to go booming out to the bunkhouse and turn out the lot of them. I roused other attention than that, too. Two or three rifles began to crack, and a whir of lead smashed every bit of glass out of that window and sent it clinking to the floor, and the big lugs thudded through the farther wall of the room.

I stepped back, and there was the Blue Jay clinging to me in a blue funk. It was queer. You wouldn't expect him to show the white feather as bad as that, and I was pretty disgusted to hear him whining: "It is no use! You cannot keep him away!"

"You damn little blockhead!" says I to the Blue Jay. "The door's locked. No use bothering about that. It will take a good deal of battering before it can possibly go down. And before that could happen, the boys will be here. D'you hear them?"

My shouting and the noise of the rifles had been enough to raise the dead, and it didn't need much of an alarm to get my punchers from the bunkhouse. I could hear them shouting as the door of the bunkhouse was rushed open. Now they were in the open, coming towards the house, and no matter who they were who were outside the house, or how many, they would have their hands full, directly.

There was only one immediate danger, so far as I could see, which was that those gents outside might swarm up the outside of the house and try to force a way through the window, but though I was a pretty bad shot, I thought that I could promise them a hot time as they climbed through into the room. So I had my Colt out and faced that way.

In the thing that followed, I've thought ever since that if I'd been alone I should have done a lot better. It was Pepillo that paralyzed me. Because although he seen what was happening before me, his way of giving me a warning was a scream that stopped the blood running in my veins and turned me numb.

I swung around—and there was my locked door swinging open and on the threshold stood a chap in a tight Mexican jacket—I saw that much—with a black mask across his face. I tried to get my gun up and fire, but I hadn't a chance. He simply twitched up the muzzle of his Colt and fired from the hip. That's the fastest way, of course, only usually the gent that fires from the hip breaks the window or ploughs up the ceiling. But this time it was different. That bullet clipped me alongside the head. It was a feeling as if a red-hot knife had ploughed its way along my scalp, and at the same time, a hammer seemed to hit me. I dropped into blackness and didn't feel the floor as I struck it. I was out, completely.

But I wasn't out more than a second. When I scrambled to my knees, there was the scent of burning powder in my nostrils, and the house was rocking with an uproar. I ran out into the hallway, and looking down the stairs, I saw Pepillo in the arms of a gent who was carrying him through the front door—the same gent that had stood in the door of my room and shot me down.

How could I recognize him for sure? Because there was something light and fast and strong about him that spoke to me as surely as though I had seen the face behind the mask.

I started down the steps five at a time, and the gent in the Mexican jacket turned and let me have it again.

The dark was against him. His bullet winged right past my cheek, but it was a clean miss, no matter how close.

His second shot would have killed me, I suppose, but he never had a chance to fire a second one. As he swung to shoot, two forms heaved into the doorway, one as big as myself, and the other short and squat. I knew them in spite of having only moonshine to see them by—Shorty and Rusty McArdle! And there was never a more welcome sight to any man's eyes.

They caught the stranger as a wave catches a box, and picked him up and carried him before them. By the time that I got down there, the work was over. Pepillo was crouched in a corner, with a hand across his eyes as though he was trying to shut out terrible sights and terrible thoughts. And here was the stranger with big Rusty standing behind him, holding his hands so that he could not move.

Says the stranger, in very good English: "Your man is breaking my wrists, señor. Will you ask him to stop?"

There was no need for brutality. Shorty had frisked the chap in the jacket and got his knife and his guns—two pairs! So I passed Rusty the word to get a Colt out and keep it out, and to keep in his place behind the stranger; and in the meantime, I had another job on my hands, because the house niggers and the cowpunchers were flocking into the place, and here was young Randal and old Randal coming down the steps, four at a time.

Old Henry Randal walks up to the stranger, whose mask had been took off by Shorty.

"Pablo Almadares!" says he. "On my soul and body, it's Pablo Almadares!"

I knew that he was right, too. That fellow was so handsome, so graceful and so easy, that you could tell that he was a fighter. He had his head up, and his big black eyes was as calm as you please while he looked us over.

Only, when they lighted on me, a flash came across them, like a glint of red fire in a glass, and his lips straightened out a little. It made me back up, that look did. The way a dog backs up when a wolf snarls. I herded the cowpunchers out of the house, by telling them that some of the pals of Almadares were still outside of the house, and they ought to nab them.

Now that they had Pablo, they were keen to round up some of the rest of the gang, and they left *pronto*. After that, I had to push the niggers out of the room. That left Harry and Henry Randal and Shorty and Rusty and Pepillo, besides Pablo and me.

Everybody was feeling pretty gay. All except Pepillo and Almadares. It was a queer thing to see the kid cowering in the corner, and watching that Almadares as though he had been hypnotized, and never so much as looking at me, or asking me if my head was bad hurt, while Rusty clipped the hair away and swabbed me with iodine that burned in like sixty and set my whole brain on fire.

As for Shorty, he sat down with a long gun in each hand, and his eyes was fair blazing as they studied that outlaw. He never moved his eyes and he never moved his guns, but if Almadares leaned forward a little, one of Shorty's guns would lean forward along with him; and if Pablo straightened in his chair, one of Shorty's guns would straighten, too.

There was enough reward for that fellow to make one cowpuncher pretty rich, and even though Shorty and Rusty would have to divide the reward between them, still there would be what you might call plenty for each of them. Shorty was enjoying the taste of that money beforehand, but he wasn't allowing his day dreams to come between him and the facts. He forgot everything in the world except the fact that Pablo Almadares meant just as much money dead as he did alive—and my, my, but Shorty wanted a good excuse to make him good and safe and dead!

That left the Randals. Harry Randal was sort of sunning himself in the firelight of good fortune, as you might say. He lolled back in his chair and smoked a cigarette, blowing the smoke very lazy and sort of insulting towards his grandfather.

"It sort of looks, grandfather," says Harry, "that I'm going to win the bargain, after all! It sort of looks, grandfather, as though I had stopped up the rustling leak right at the source. There'll be no more trouble now that we have the head of the gang. With this Almadares fellow out of the way, the rustlers are going to shun Sour Creek Valley as though it were loaded with poison. Am I right, Pablo?"

Almadares smiled.

"Señor, you compliment very highly; oh, very highly indeed, my friend!' says that calm crook.

Old Henry Randal, he starts walking up and down the room in his pyjamas and his slippers, packing his little clay pipe tight and then lighting it, and leaving behind him a trail of tobacco smoke so strong that even Shorty blinked when some of it blew his way.

"Now, take it all in all," says Henry Randal, "I have to confess that matters are not turning out as they *should* have turned out. In the first place, there's the mysterious fact that the cows increase over night—"

"You'd simply failed to see a herd of them packed away into one of the gullies," says Harry, very bland.

The old chap turned around and shot one glance at him.

"Young man," says he, "I want you to know that I never fail to see *anything* when seeing is what I'm out to do. But overlooking the cows, let's get down to another thing. What in the devil could have made this Pablo Almadares want to kidnap a worthless and unknown brat like this Pepillo, will you tell me? Almadares, will you tell me what's the value of this brat?"

Almadares puts back his head, and he smiles at me.

"Perhaps Señor Kitchin can tell us the secret value," says he.

"Kitchin, Kitchin?" barks Henry Randal, not missing a trick. "Is that your real name, Smith-Jones?"

I shrugged my shoulders.

"You do not know?" says Almadares, lifting his eyebrows very wicked, and still showing his teeth in that true Mexican smile of his.

"Kitchin?" says Henry Randal. "It seems to me that I heard of a prospector by name of Kitchin making a strike. Almadares, where does this Kitchin hail from?"

"From Fulsom Prison, for the past two years," says Almadares.

"Fulsom Prison!" says Henry Randal.

"Fulsom!" gasps Shorty and Rusty in one breath.

And then Henry Randal begins to laugh.

"Ah, well," says he, "I guessed one-half of the story before it was told. Don't look so downhearted, Harry. The main thing is to have a man who can run your ranch and who can run it well, and so long as you have the right man for that, can't you overlook his record?"

"Thanks, Pablo," says I. "I won't forget!"

"Señor," says he, with a lot of emotion, "this is nothing compared with what I should like to do for you!"

"All right," says Henry Randal, "but still I should like to know what about Pepillo, yonder, has made you risk your life, Almadares, in a crazy way like this!"

"I tell you the truth," said Almadares. "I thought that Señor Kitchin would fight like an honest—murderer. I did not dream that he would ever call for help and bring his men—"

"Well," says Henry Randal, "for that mistake you'll hang, my young friend Almadares."

Almadares' smile didn't waver a fraction of a second.

"Hang?" gasps Pepillo. "Hang?" And he jumps to his feet.

Almadares stood up, too, and laid his hand on his heart, and bowed very low.

"Certainly I shall hang," says he. "And for all of this, I thank you, my dear friend!"

"Pablo," says Shorty behind his guns, "you pretty near escaped hanging, then; and if you jump up again like that you *will* die with your boots on. Because I'll kill you, son, as sure as you're an inch high."

"Mind the kid," says Rusty. "He's fainting!"

CHAPTER XXXI

I thought that he *would* drop, for a minute, but when I stepped to him, Pepillo turned and give me a look of hate and scorn and disgust that stopped me short. And then he turned around and walked right out of the room. I glanced at this Almadares, and the very first thing that I seen was that his eyes was not black after all, but a very dark brown; exactly like the eyes of Pepillo. And at that, an explanation of everything jumped through my mind. It was so clear that fire couldn't have been truer. It was so bright a truth that it dazzled me.

I says, rather husky: "Shorty, I want you to put this Almadares down in the same room where young Dance was kept. Put him down there, and you and Rusty keep turns guarding him. You might as well stay at the mouth of the tunnel, because there's nothing but the side passage that leads to the room besides that one hallway; and the door to the passage is rusted as thick as the devil and I have the key to it. But keep a tight watch on him, and keep your ears open! You understand?"

I didn't have to say that. I knew that they *would* understand. And I started for the door.

Old Henry Randal pipes up and says: "Kitchin!"

I turned to him.

"Kitchin," says he, "I don't want you to think that I respect you any the less. Matter of fact, I have *more* respect for a crook who has paid the penalty for at least part of his crimes than I have for one who has come off scot-free!"

I didn't want his good opinion. I went on out of that room and I climbed the stairs slowly, with a pulse of blood jumping into the wound in my head with every step that I took. It seemed as though the pain helped to make me think clearly, though. It seemed as though I could be sure of what I saw now.

I got up to my room, and there was my Pepillo sitting with his elbows on the center table and his face in his hands, pretty near spent. When the door closed, he didn't so much as look up. I laid a hand on his shoulder. He shrugged it off with a little gasp of disgust.

"I ain't a beast, kid," says I. "And I got no call to be used like this by you. I got no call to be used like this at all, and you ought to know it! But I understand, Pepillo. Poor kid! Everything is clear to me at last; I understand perfect!"

He dropped his hands and looked at me, sort of half scared and half bewildered.

"You understand?" says he.

I nodded at him, and then I explained: "I noticed that his eyes were the same color as yours. That gave me the first clue. And then I could see, Blue Jay, that he had the same sort of a graceful way about him—and he looks slim and light, but very strong, just the way that you will be when you grow up—and so that's why I could see the truth about the pair of you."

"Be quick and simple," says Pepillo, and he half-closed his eyes, and I saw how really white his face was. "Be quick and be simple, in the name of God, for I have no strength to work riddles, to-night."

"You don't have to," says I. "You don't have to, poor kid. But I tell you, that I understand everything. It was Almadares that sent the cattle down into the valley. Ain't that right?"

By his quick start, I knew that it *was* right, though he didn't speak.

"And he sent down the cattle because you sent word to him to *ask* them from him; and that was why you turned loose Sammy Dance!"

Pepillo went back a step and with a hand pressed against his face, he stared at me in a sort of horror.

"How have you come to guess at these things, señor?" says he.

"Because I finally guessed at the main secret," says I. "You are—the brother of Pablo Almadares!"

Pepillo left the wall with a lurch and covered his eyes

with his hands. He was so choked that I didn't wait for him to speak.

"Sit down, kid," says I, "and I'll tell you what I've done. I've told Shorty to put Almadares in the same room where Sammy Dance was kept. And I've told them to keep guard at the end of the hall. There's another way to the little corner cellar room where Almadares will be kept, and that passage ends in a door that's never used, and the lock is filled with rust. But here's the key to it, Pepillo, and oil will soften rust. If you squirt that lock full of oil and wait ten minutes, chances are that you can turn that lock without making a sound. Then go down and turn your brother loose."

Pepillo tried to speak, but there was too much in him to come out in words. He made a gesture with both hands, and then I says: "Take it easy for half an hour or so, and then start work. I'm going out for a walk!"

I left the room and went out into the night.

The whole thing looked pretty good to me. I would be turning that Almadares loose, and he looked to me like pretty much of a white man. He hated me, of course, because he thought that I had kept his brother away from him, but now that I was turning him free, he would get over that. When Pepillo told him what I had done; instead of a dead rustler, we would have a rustler in the mountains that would be a friend to the ranch, and that would be better still.

It was certainly a wicked look that this Almadares had given me when he was in the living-room, but that was all explained, now, to my satisfaction, and time passed pretty fast for me as I walked under the trees in front of the house.

I went around and had a look at the bunkhouse. The boys were having a pretty gay time, now, and they were whooping it up in great style. Bright as the moon was—and it stood at the full right in the center of the sky—the light from the bunkhouse windows went a step or two into the night, and it showed me half a dozen ponies tied up in front of the bunkhouse. Those fellows inside were not taking anything for granted, and if there were more trouble this night, they had their ponies ready to follow it, hot-foot.

Maybe I had been walking around for about an hour. Anyway, the lights were out in the bunkhouse, and the

chill of the night air was beginning to make the fresh
wound in my head ache. And then a gun crackled from
the house, and I heard two voices booming out: the voice
of Shorty and the voice of Rusty McArdle!

I saw as much as I heard, too. For yonder, close to the
bunkhouse, I saw two figures running: Pepillo, without
any doubt, and his brother, Pablo Almadares, along side
of him. They grabbed two of the tethered horses, and they
was off in a minute. And here was Rusty and Shorty
swarming after them, as hard as they could sprint.

That was more than I had bargained for. I should have
thought that if Pepillo wanted to go away with his brother,
he would of told me so before he started. I had given him
plenty of chance. Still, I didn't want them followed, and I
hurried along to stop Rusty and Shorty if I could.

When I come up, Rusty was in the saddle already, and
Shorty was hauling away at the knot that tied another
hoss. He seen me and he yelled: "They're away! Pablo
and the girl, both of them."

It come through me like another bullet. I grabbed
Shorty and I jammed his back against the wall of the
bunkhouse, while the boys was piling out of the place.

"Girl?" says I to Shorty. "Did you say, girl?"

There was plenty of moonshine to show me his face,
and there was more wonder in it than excitement, that
minute.

"My God," says Shorty, "you mean to say that all this
time—and you didn't know? You didn't know?"

I knew, then! Oh, it was clean enough what a dundering
idiot and blockhead I had been! Seemed to me, then, that
I should have known on the very first day, by the look
of the small, soft feet of the kid that I met in front of
Gregorio's shop. And it seemed to me that I should of
knowed by the sound of the voice, that was softer and
sweeter than even a boy's had any right to be. I should of
knowed by a thousand other things, too. And most of all
—oh, what a fool, a fool I had been!—I should have
known by the face of the ghost that had come to me in
the middle of the night!

Seeing it now with new eyes, as I raced a horse through
the night with Rusty and Shorty ahead of me, I knew that
from the first there had been something familiar about
that face. The face of the boy—the face of Pepillo! And
not that of Stephen Randal's dead wife at all!

And besides, would any man have done for a mere brother what Pablo Almadares was willing to do for this girl?

It was clear as bright midday. This was Leonor Mauricio who had run away from her father to escape from that promised marriage to Pablo Almadares. But he had won after all and in spite of all. She had sold herself a second time for my sake, to bring the cattle into the valley. And now she was keeping her promise in fact, and riding away with him—

Rusty, keeping the lead, had swung onto the upper road that led along the creek. That was the way that the fugitives had taken. Yes, and through the moonlight it seemed to me that I could see them galloping.

I was the last of the three, because my horse was a little slower, though it was strong as a devil beneath me. But still, I was leading the mob of cowpunchers who were following the same trail far behind me.

They were too far away. It was up to the three of us, and somehow I felt a prophecy in me that I should come to grips with this Almadares before the night was ended, and one of us should die and one of us should live for the sake of Leonor—Pepillo—the Blue Jay!

Ay, Blue Jay was the name, but he had never before made such mischief as would follow on this night!

CHAPTER XXXII

Going down a slope, I pushed up to Shorty, and I could holler ahead to big Rusty McArdle.

"What hosses did they take, Rusty?" I yelled to him.

He turned in the saddle, without slackening his pace. "Dan Murphy's grey and the bald-faced boy mare!"

Then two names knocked nine-tenths of my hopes out from under me, because the both of them animals was pretty well known to us on the ranch for speed. Besides, here was the three of us, all on more than average cowponies, to be sure, but all of us heavyweights of the rankest kind. And yonder there was Pepillo—somehow, I couldn't think of her by any other name!—and young Pablo Almadares; the both of them lightweights, and of course Pepillo in particular.

No, it didn't look like we had much chance, but still, no matter what I might think, there was the fact of the matter: that the two of them didn't seem to draw no further ahead of me.

"Lame!" yells Shorty at my ear. "Lame, by God, one of them!"

That must of been it, of course. Yes, and in another moment there was a glint of a hoss ahead of us, and we went crashing past the bald-faced mare. We spurred on, then, with Shorty and Rusty pulling well into the lead, and as they rode, they yelled like a couple of Indians on a blood trail—and a blood trail they sure intended to make it.

Far ahead of us, we saw a flash and there was the grey horse, straining hard and carrying his double load very fast—but never fast enough. Oh, we could see them wonderful clear in that bright moonlight, but that demon Almadares could see us, just as well. I saw the wink of his rifle as he turned. He fired, and there was Shorty doubled up in the saddle.

I pulled up beside him.

"Shorty, are you bad hurt!" says I.

"You damned fool!" says Shorty. "Ride like hell, and get him for me! Don't waste time on me!"

I didn't wait to be asked twice. A man can't leave a pal that's wounded, of course, not unless he's told to go on, but how I blessed Shorty for letting me keep on that trail; because still there was a sort of a voice in me, saying that before the end I would sure have this out with Almadares, hand to hand!

We climbed a long slope, and at the head of it, Rusty had pressed well ahead of me, and he was wonderfully close to that Almadares and the grey. I yelled for Rusty to rein back and to let me come up and we'd both close in on them, but Rusty wanted to have the glory of this all for himself. He spurred and quirted his hoss ahead, with a revolver cocked out in front of him.

What good was that? How could he shoot, when there was the girl right in the arms of Almadares, as you might say? No, he could only bluff, and Almadares was not the kind that could be bluffed out particularly easy, I can tell you!

That long rifle swung about and steadied to a mere point of light. Rusty McArdle pitched from his saddle and lay in a horrible heap on the ground; and as he fell, the explosion of the rifle rang like a beating hammer in my ear.

I didn't wait to ask questions; because I figured that Rusty was sure a dead man, or a dying. I jumped from the saddle and kneeled by him.

"Big Boy!" gasps Rusty.

"Ay," says I. "It's me, Rusty. What'll you have? Where did the slug hit you?"

"It missed me—I mean, it only grazed me," says Rusty. "Take my hoss, Big Boy—he's better than yours—and ride, ride, for God's sake. She's too good for any Mexican dog!"

This was what Rusty McArdle says, as he lies there, bleeding fast. I listened, and away off behind me, I thought that I could hear the trampling of the hosses coming up the pass, and I says to myself that the rest of the boys would be there pretty quick. But oh, while I was trying to tell myself that, I dropped a hand on the breast of Rusty, and it was sopping wet with blood, and I knew right well where my duty and my conscience lay.

Rusty was saying: "What are you waiting for? You damned thick-head, you was always sort of half stupid! I'm only grazed; skin broke, and that's all. Ride on, partner. You'll never get at him from behind. You got to cut ahead and try to rush him down The Slide. That's the only way. Go on, Big Boy! Good luck if you go, and damn you for a welcher if you stay here. Are you afraid of his gun?"

That was what Rusty said, gasping the words out, and trying to make himself sneer at me, to sting me along. Only, the pain was so terrible that he couldn't control himself, and the sneer turned into an awful gaping.

I looked around me and if ever a man asked God to tell him what was the right thing to do, it was me as I kneeled there. Up the valley of Sour Creek was Almadares carrying Pepillo into hell; and here was Rusty McArdle dying for lack of a bunkie's help.

I say that I looked around me, but I didn't get no help. There was only the whiteness and the brightness of Sour Creek under the moon, and there was some willows hanging their black heads against the silver of the water, and an owl with a voice like a loon went over our heads.

"My hoss is better than yours," says Rusty. "Will you take him, Big Boy? I've been a damned poor sort of a man!"

Well, maybe you think that was a funny thing for him to say, but I suppose that while Rusty lay there, feeling the life drip out of him, he got a flash of everything that he had been. And every man has got a feeling that he owes something, I dunno to what. He had never paid in his life, and he hoped to pay with his death.

Anyway, I grabbed his hand, with no word to say to him. Then I jumped into the saddle on his hoss, and I drove that pony straight into the hills. He was right. It was a better mount than the one that I had had. I could tell it by the life in his haunches as he drove and lifted me up the first slope. But I saved him a little. There was no use killing his strength in that first effort. Up above was where he needed his strength.

You see, the road along Sour Creek was the fastest and the easiest grade for going up the valley towards the south mountains. But right here Sour Creek made a big swing, going through the first steep-sided hills, and what Rusty had suggested was that I should cut across the cord of the arc that the creek made and so come out at the straight, again. At that place was what we called The Slide, because there was a long, smooth gravelled fall of ground that dropped from the head of the rise right down to the trail that went along the bank of the river. When I got to the top of the plateau, I turned that hoss loose and I bit into him with spur and quirt, and I jockeyed him along, easing myself into the stirrups. That was a time for saving ground, too, because when I come out at the top of The Slide, I could see Pablo Almadares and the girl rocking along at the laboring canter of their hoss, rocking along like a pair of shadows against the whiteness of Sour Creek under the moon.

My pony tried to balk at the edge of the slope, but I fair lifted him over the edge, and after that, the fall of the ground did the rest. The mustang laid back his ears and squatted, and down we went with a rush. We knocked loose a shower of pebbles and rock that went leaping down the Slide before us.

Even if Almadares hadn't had the eye of a hawk, that rattle of rocks would have told him what was coming. I heard a wild, shrill cry coming through the wind: "Señor, go back!" That was Pepillo, telling me that it was sure death to come on—and I felt it was death, too; felt it right in my bones; but it was a lot too late to turn back, now. The fall of the ground had taken charge of me, and as I went down it on wings, a sort of crazy enthusiasm got hold on me.

I saw Almadares halt; I saw his rifle pitch up to his shoulder; and that was to be the end of me, I thought. No, it was Pepillo that knocked the barrel of the rifle up.

Almadares put his politeness in his pocket. He turned and threw Pepillo to the ground, and there she lay, stunned, while he jerked up his rifle again. I had come down in a swirl of dust and dirt and flying pebbles right to the trail along the edge of the Creek, and now I got the staggering pony righted and drove full at the Mexican with my revolver barking as fast as I could pull the trigger.

Ay, but how was I to do any execution from the back of a galloping horse? The rifle went up again to the shoulder of Almadares. I saw a spurt of flame, and a heavy weight struck my breast and tore through me. It jerked me a little around in the saddle, and it turned my body numb, but my arms and my hands were still alive. As I came flying in, a roar like a beast came out of my throat, and I threw the revolver. It hit the rifle, not Pablo, but it turned his last shot wild, and the next second I was at him.

I couldn't spare the time or the hand for reining in the pony. I just reached for Almadares as we went by and I caught him around the body. The shock dragged us from our hosses. We went down with a smash, me undermost, with the feeling that I had a fighting wild-cat and not a man in my hands. He tried to claw loose, but his effort only pulled me to my feet, still with a hold on him.

Ay, I was on my feet, but the last of my strength was going fast. I couldn't last to throttle him. My body was turning into the weakness of water, and a red-hot sword was plunging through my breast, drawing out, and plunging through again, while the hot blood trickled down front and back. But I still had my arms and my hands.

"Almadares," says I, "will you give up to me, on your honor?"

"Gringo dog!" snarls Almadares, and tries to claw out his knife.

I lifted him above my head. The sway of him sent me staggering, like I was drunk, but I managed to throw him away, and he dropped like a stone, reaching vainly at me as he fell.

He turned over in the air. There was a horrible, soft, crunching sound as he struck a flat-faced rock beside the water. Then he slipped off into the current and went sliding down Sour Creek. That was what I saw before the blackness walked across my eyes. I turned around, trying to feel my way.

"Pepillo!" says I. "The moon has got behind a cloud—where are you?"

I couldn't make out what it was that come for answer, but I closed my arms and found the softness of a woman inside of them. What did I care, then, for what might come afterwards?

CHAPTER XXXIII

Have you ever been so sick that you enjoyed the fever and the weakness, like water, humming up and down your veins? That was the way with me. And when I come out of the shadows, the first time of all, I remember that there was a flare of sun, and on the edge of my bed against the sun there was a girl sitting in a blue dress, with black hair, and a clear olive skin, and eyes browner than the shadows under oak trees. I reached out a hand as the darkness begun to swing across my eyes. My hand was caught in slim, cold fingers.

"Big boy!"

"Pepillo!" says I, and as I went out, again, there was a ghost of perfume in my nostrils—jasmine!

When I come out of the dark again, I was stronger. The dreams that I had been having was happier dreams, and now when I turned my head I seen that it was twilight, and right beside my bed, in a chair all piled with pillows, was the Blue Jay, with her head turned towards me, smiling in her sleep, and looking so wonderful beautiful and happy and kind that I had to close my eyes quick to keep it from being too much for me.

I slept that night nacheral and deep, and when I wakened in the sunrise time, I had strength back in me, and I says to Pepillo: "Blue Jay, what the devil should I be calling you? I ask your pardon for swearing!"

She was sitting cross-legged on the broad arm of that chair, though how she ever managed, you would have to ask her. And she grinned at me. It was a wonderful relief to find that Pepillo still could grin like that even after getting to be a woman.

"You need not call me Leonor," says she, "but I should like to know your own name," she says. "I think that I really *ought* to, don't you?"

I closed my eyes.

"You will laugh like the devil, it's so silly," says I.

"I will not laugh, like a devil," says Pepillo. "Tell me!"

"It's Percival!" says I, groaning. "Percival Kitchin—and that's the truth, though you wouldn't never believe it, to look at me."

It was a grand thing, I tell you, to hear her laugh, and to see her rocking back and forth like a bird on a branch.

"Big Boy," says she, "it's a wonderful joke, isn't it? But isn't it the devil to have to grow up in one day?"

"Blue Jay," says I, "as long as there is trouble to make, you'll make it. And as for growing up in one day, it won't happen as long as you live."

"Well," says the Blue Jay, cocking her head on one side, "I am going to have to mollycoddle you, when you come home at night, after working all day?"

"Blue Jay," says I, "whenever you try to pet me, I'll know that you're laughing behind my back, you devil!"

"Hush!" says Pepillo. "Do you not see that I am so foolish, and I love you so much, that I tremble at being near you?"

"Are you laughing at me, Pepillo?" says I. "Because I wouldn't trust you, you mocking devil!"

"Ah, my dear," says she. "But I know nothing whatever about oil paintings."

"Oil paintings be damned," says I.

"Hush!" says Pepillo. "Because I think that Shorty will hear you swearing at me, Big Boy."

"Shorty!" says I. And I tried to pull myself up on my elbows, but Pepillo took me by the shoulders and pressed me back, dead easy.

And there's Shorty, looking pretty white, but grinning pretty near broader than human and looking so Godawful ugly, which you wouldn't believe it.

"Seems like you found somebody strong enough to handle you, at last," says Shorty. "Seems like you're beat, Big Boy. A life decision is what Pepillo has got over you."

"Pepillo," says I, "beat it, will you?"

She went out onto the balcony outside of the room, and she begun to sing there, not loud enough to drown out our talk, but just so's the sweetness of her voice, it come tangling like flowers through our words.

"Now, Shorty," says I, "what I want to know—"

Shorty put up his hand and he got a little whiter than before.

"It was no good, Big Boy," says he. "We done what we could, but he didn't seem to care to fight, none. He bucked up till he heard that you had got Almadares good, and that Pepillo was safe, and that you was gunna live through it, and then he closed his eyes. 'That,' says Rusty McArdle, 'is enough. Boys, I got one thing to ask. When I die, I want to be planted down here by the side of Sour Creek. Because this here is the place—I never paid when I entered—but I'm glad to pay going out!' That was the way that he died! He let go all holts!"

What would become of a gent like Big Boy? Well, I dunno. I would be afraid to ask a preacher, y'understand, but I would bet on Rusty's outside chance, so long as he was in the race. He was a clean fighter, was Rusty.

God bless him!

Says Pepillo: "Now, what a silly way to end up your history, without saying any of the really important things!"

"Like what?" says I.

"Why, about the ranch. Do you want them to think that you own the Sour Creek place, Big Boy?"

No, of course I don't. What busted things was that Harry Randal got too confident and too much up in the air about what was gunna be his, and before his probation time was up he got into a gambling game that nicked him for enough thousands to put the ranch in the hole very deep and bad. He lost his hope of his grandfather's millions, right there.

But how comes it that we are still back on the Sour Creek ranch? I'll tell you. I had ought to ask the pardon of Henry Randal for the way that I've been talking about him, but I've put down everything in black and white, just as the ideas run into my head at the time that they was happening. However, when Harry's debts run up bog and he had to sell in, it was Henry Randal that bought in the place for a song, and then he sent for me and installed me here as boss—but not on a salary: on shares, and doggone fat shares, too!

"I like the way that you make fires," says Henry Randal. "You use big sticks!"

"Well," says Pepillo, "is that all?"

"Now, Blue Jay," says I, looking up to her and shaking my head, "what the devil else could there be to write about? Ain't I said nearly everything that there is in the world?"

"Silly Big Boy!" says Pepillo. "Don't you see that you've left the most important thing of all out?"

"What might that be?" says I.

She only laughs at me.

"Listen!" says she.

I listen, and off there in the distance there is the yapping of a couple of kids on the lawn, where they're rolling, and getting covered with sunburn, and dust, and dead leaves, and what-not.

"There!" says Pepillo. "Put that in, won't you?"

But how can I put it in, as I sit here looking up to her, and studying how much happiness and brightness there is in her, and how much sadness, too, in loving a girl that is so far beyond me. But these here things that are gifts from the Gods, they ain't given according to merit, but just according to chance, of course.

The wind blows the lowing of the cows up the Sour Creek valley, and the wind stirs the vine that climbs across the window, but I think that nothing that it carries to me means so much as the breath of the jasmine that we've planted there below, in the garden.